Through My Daughter's Eyes

Julia Dye

based on a story by
Dallas Burgess

WARRIORS PUBLISHING GROUP
NORTH HILLS, CALIFORNIA

THROUGH MY DAUGHTER'S EYES

A Warriors Publishing Group book/published by arrangement with the author

PRINTING HISTORY
Warriors Publishing Group December 2017

ISBN: 978-1-944353-14-8

Library of Congress Control Number: 2017915725

The name "Warriors Publishing Group" and the logo
are trademarks belonging to Warriors Publishing Group

PRINTED IN THE UNITED STATES OF AMERICA

10 9 8 7 6 5 4 3 2 1

Not all those who wander are lost

—J. R. R. Tolkien

ometimes we want something in our life to matter so much that we make the things that happened matter far more than they deserve.

Sometimes the things that really matter we don't find out about until much later.

This is the thing that mattered.

A tactical vehicle rumbled by, metal clanging. The radio beeped.

Aaron said, "Echo Base, Storm Chaser Seven, over."

"Storm Chaser Seven, this is Echo Base. Send your traffic."

"Roger, Storm Chaser. Element approaching phase line alpha. How copy, over?"

"Echo Base copies. Phase line alpha."

Dad had a photograph inside the HUMVEE of a little girl with blonde hair and blue eyes, and its wrinkled and worn edges shook as the tactical vehicle chugged down the street. My picture.

BOOM!

The vehicle stopped and so did the shakiness. The HUMVEE right in front of him had hit an Improvised Explosive Device.

"Storm Chaser 3, Storm Chaser 3, this is Storm Chaser 7; over…" said my dad.

"7, this is Storm Chaser 3."

"Roger. Storm Chaser 2 is down, I say again, Storm Chaser 2 is down…break…I need you to secure the rear as we move forward to assess casualties, over…" he replied.

"Roger that." Someone was shooting at them, making a sound like popcorn. My dad got out of their vehicle along with some other soldiers. The popcorn sound grew deeper, like a thumping heart.

When my dad got to the blown-up vehicle, the front-passenger door had been blown open. He reached in and dragged out a soldier, crying, "Medic!" The soldier was really hurt.

Once the medic arrived, running, he pushed my dad out of the way and started to examine the wounded guy. Dad returned to his own radio—and my wrinkled photo.

"Echo Base, Echo Base, this is Storm Chaser 7, over."

"Storm Chaser 7, go for Echo Base."

"Echo Base, our lead vehicle had been struck by an IED and had taken casualties. Prepare to copy nine-line medevac." A nine-line is used for calling in a combat injury. When someone you know gets hurt, it can be stressful and hectic, and it's used to calmly and accurately report that a soldier needs medical attention. My dad was ready to give all the important information so that the guy could get help.

"Echo Base copies. Go ahead with nine-line."

Something popped and hissed. "RPG!" someone shouted. A rocket-propelled grenade was bad news.

My dad looked at my picture one more time. The hiss grew louder, until a flash of light obliterated his vision.

My dad lived. And he was sorry.

2

ooking back, I can see that what led up to that moment began when I was just a kid at Dessau Middle School—go Diamondbacks! Seriously, what school has a snake for a mascot? Felt like I was in Slytherin House.

It was the dreaded School Picture Day. I lined up with all the other 7th graders in my class outside the library, and we went in one by one to prove to our relatives that we were complete geeks. Sure, I had the obligatory blonde hair and blue eyes for your typical fairy princess, but I also had the body of a 10-year-old boy and although the bright orange shirt I'd worn was my favorite, it clashed desperately with the photographer's ridiculous magenta backdrop.

When it was my turn to be humiliated, I perched on the rickety stool and tried to smile. After the flash seared into my eyeballs—likely inflicting permanent damage—I blinked and stumbled my way back past the line as the next kid moved into the shrine of doom.

As I walked down the empty hallway, lined with lockers, the school day-ending bell rung and classroom doors opened flinging students out like doves at a wedding ceremony. Some went to their lockers, others walked in groups, and a few clumps stood around. You know, the cool kids. I grabbed Megan, my friend and co-conspirator in our plot to be just good enough to not get noticed and not so good that we'd be picked out for any attention. You move a lot when you're an Army brat, and we'd both learned to keep silhouettes from the skyline.

We ran home through the gorgeous spring weather. Texas can be beautiful, especially at the edge of hill country. Our minds were on summer vacation and the possibility of getting away for a while. We're both huge fans of *parkour*—running over, around, and through obstacles to get quickly from one place to another. It's about efficiency. Table in the way? Vault over it! How about a log? Crawl under it. The idea is to get from one place to another in the most direct way possible, regardless of what's in your way. Sometimes you have to be really creative.

We clambered over a fence that was blocking the shortest way to my house. Megan was talking about this cool summer camp she was attending. "Yeah, it's going to be my first time away from home that long," she said. "You should ask your parents if you can come."

"I will, but I think we're going somewhere this summer."

"Where?"

"I don't know yet."

Once we reached my house, I stopped while Megan continued walking on all fours like an orangutan, toes and fingertips on the ground. "I'll see you tomorrow!" she shouted.

"Bye!" I cried. I turned and walked up the sidewalk leading to the front door and entered, setting my backpack by the front door. Our house was a large two-story deal in Harris Ridge. I walked through the family room to the kitchen. Standing there, eating a Pop-Tart over the sink and reading the paper, was a man in DCU trousers, a light tan undershirt, and desert-suede combat boots.

"Daddy!" I cried, running up to him. He knelt to reach me and I jumped into his arms. He smelled like wet grass and wood smoke. "You're home!"

"Yeah, they let us go early today."

My mom walked into the kitchen, breaking up our happy moment. My mom's pretty, like blonde hair and blue eyes are supposed to look.

"I would hope so," said Mom. "It should be illegal to have y'all in the field so long when the weather is this beautiful." She went to the fridge to evaluate our dinner options. Probably something healthy and disgusting. I eyed the Frosted Cherry Pop-Tart on the counter with renewed respect. I plopped myself down on a stool while Dad stood up and turned to our Healthy Choice chef.

"You speak the truth, my Queen," he said. He put his hands on her waist and kissed her neck. She closed her eyes a bit and smiled, then he leaned back against the counter. "And being such that it is, I, for one, suggest that we vacate this humble abode and venture forth into said beautiful weather and fatten our bellies with deep-fried avocado!" Texans can chicken-fry anything.

He stood up straight and tall as if he were a knight, making me giggle. My hero; knight sometimes, other times a teddy bear made of pudding.

Mom turned and shut the refrigerator. "And I, for one, agree—since we don't really have anything to cook anyway."

"Then it is settled." Dad grabbed Mom around the waist, pulled her close, and held out an arm, welcoming me to the family embrace. "Onward!"

Mom pulled him back by his tan undershirt. "You're not going anywhere in that stinky thing."

He bent down towards me and whispered, "The knight must now go as a pauper."

"You're always a knight!" I cried. He stood back up, tall, regaining his regal stature.

"My lady," he said, bowing once again, to me this time.

As he left the kitchen, he pinched Mom's butt causing her to squeal and jump. She turned and glared at me, but I just giggled back.

3

ince it was such a pretty evening, we sat on the patio at The Roaring Fork. They do wood-fired cooking that's absolutely delicious. It's my favorite place to eat. Their service is pretty decent, too. The patio overlooks Quarry Lake, and though the view was a bit obstructed by the trees, we got to see one of Austin's glorious sunsets. I ordered the Green Mac-n-Cheese while we all gobbled down the fried avocado with crab. Beats a kale salad any day of the week.

As I ate, I contemplated how to talk my way into a decent summer for once. "So, Megan was telling me about this summer camp she's going to, and she keeps asking me to go," I finally said.

Dad replied, "Yeah? When is it?"

"It starts in June."

"How long is it?" asked Mom.

"I'm not too sure. I'll ask."

"Well, keep in mind that we are going on a little summer vacation in June," said Dad. "I've got some leave built up and want to go before summer gets unbearable." The disappointment must have shown on my face. "Tell you what. Your mom and I will talk to Megan's parents and get some details, and we'll go from there. Deal?"

That was more encouraging. "Deal."

Dad put down his fork and extended his arm over the table offering only his pinky. I reached out and we locked pinkies in a pinky swear.

Then the Mac-n-Cheese arrived and I forgot everything else. After that, we split a chocolate torte with fresh strawberries and cinnamon roll icing and I lost all cognitive thought.

After dinner, I retreated to my bedroom, which is extraordinary. It's large and I'm allowed to decorate as I wish, as long as it's sanitary, tidy, and if I wear a helmet if I'm going to climb. It's silly because the walls aren't that high—high for a bedroom but not high for a climb—but it's not worth another fight.

My bed looks like it's suspended from the wall with climbing rope and carabiners. I've got outdoor scenes to look at, and gymnastic rings hanging from the ceiling. Dad had to put those in to be sure they'd take my weight. I've got rock-climbing holds up one wall and some bars so I can swing across the entire room. Plus there's a sliding pole down to the floor in case I don't feel like climbing down. It's epic. It also shares a wall with my parent's room. Sometimes that sucks.

Lying on the floor, thinking and digesting, I could hear them getting ready for bed. They weren't saying anything, which usually means there's tension. Kind of like that feeling you get outside before a storm.

Finally, Mom spoke. "What's on your mind?"

"You know me too well."

"Well, you've been quiet ever since we left dinner. Kind of out of it," she said. "So spill it."

"Looks like the possibility of going over is looking more like a probability. Battalion commander hadn't said anything, but Joe Rumor is running around pretty rampantly." Oh, crap. Just as I was getting used to him being home when I got home from school.

"How many of those rumors have you squashed in the last year?" she asked.

"Yeah, but this just feels different. The past five days in the field felt different."

I heard Mom plop down on the bed. "Well, I always figured it was a matter of time with all that's been going on lately."

"That's very stoic of you." I think that was kind of ironic. Mom was not ever stoic that I ever saw. Not that she ever noticed when Dad was subtle. Or me, for that matter.

"I knew what I signed up for," she continued. Dad scoffed. "What, am I a weak damsel in need of rescuing?" *Um, yes,* I thought.

"That's not it."

"Then what is it? I just want to prepare you for how hard this could be."

Mom's voice got all quivery. "I don't want it to happen. What about Abbie? How would we tell her?" Guess they didn't know that they just did. I couldn't believe that while they knew they could hear into my room—since they were always yelling for me to be quiet—that they hadn't figured out that sound moves in two directions.

He sat on her words for a moment, then said, "I don't know, either. But we have to be ready for it. I'll talk to her this weekend."

Then just silence.

On Saturday, after my morning run, I turned onto my street only to see my dad's truck parked in the driveway. He was loading fishing gear in the back. I pushed into a sprint, barreling towards him. Dad looked my way and smiled, tossing a tackle box into the cargo bed.

"Does this mean what I think it means?" I asked, putting my hands on my knees to stretch and rest.

"You betcha!"

"Is Mom going?"

"What do you think?" he replied. We both held our noses and faced each other, imitating Mom's fishing-stink-face. Then she walked out of the garage, totally not dressed to go fishing.

"Yeah, yeah, yeah," she said.

"Any chance you change your mind?" Dad asked her.

She replied, "Any chance fish have stopped smelling like fish?" Dad only laughed and turned back towards me.

"Go change. We're leaving soon." I jumped and ran into the house. Stink or no, I wanted out of there lickity-split. As I left, I heard Mom start her nag.

"You gonna talk to her?" she asked.

"Yeah, I figured this would be the best way."

I pulled on my fishing clothes: Bikini, shorts, my torn-up sheer green t-shirt, and my favorite Vans. They're green on the bottom and on the rubber around the sneaker, and the tops are red with black pips that look like seeds. Watermelon summer fishing madness. Then I grabbed a duffle with a baseball cap, sunscreen, and a hoodie in case it got cold. Sunglasses on, I was ready to roll. I sent Megan a quick text so she'd know where I was and took off downstairs. Mom had disappeared and Dad was in the driver's seat, so I popped into the passenger side.

"Don't you dare be serious today, Dad," I said, trying to ward off the conversation I knew was coming. He didn't answer, and put on some tunes. First up was

"Don't Take the Girl" by Tim McGraw. Country pretty much sucked, but there's not that many songs about fishing.

❧

We headed off towards Dessau Road towards East Pecan. When we arrived at Lake Pflugerville, Dad pulled into the parking lot and we grabbed our gear. We walked towards our favorite spot—a little micro-indentation in the lake's bank maybe 200 years north of Pier 4. I started opening the tackle box and then prepared my rod. I decided to fish with a Texas-rigged Berkley PowerWorm in Tequila Sunrise, with an eighth-ounce bullet weight.

Once we had our rods deployed, I thought I should break the ice. I knew what Dad was supposed to tell me, but he didn't know that. Waiting for him to spit it out was making my stomach churn. "What's the special occasion?" I asked.

"Do I need a special occasion to take my favorite daughter fishing?"

I rolled my eyes. "I'm your only daughter."

"All the more reason for me to spoil you." Between us, the air thickened with silence. I could practically hear his brain churning, trying to figure out what words to toss out his mouth. He took a breath. Here goes. "Actually, I did want to talk to you about something."

Enough. "It's about you leaving, isn't it?"

"Well, I'm not leaving yet," he said, surprised that I had put that bush he wanted to beat around out of its misery.

"But you might. I know a lot of other units are already gone." I wanted to storm off, toss my rod, do something dramatic. War is like that. Everything feels like a drama. Not a one of these soldiers—including my dad—had any idea what might happen. The only thing I could fit in my head was the absolute worst-case scenario. It stinks. I hate not being able to be a part of things, to help. He has to go get shot at and what do I do? Sit in school, go to the basement if there's an emergency? I don't even really understand his job in the Army. "What are you going to do?"

Dad spit into the lake, like he had a bad taste in his mouth. "Whatever I have to."

"Is it like what's on the news?" I took a deep shuddering breath. "What if you get hurt? What if you die?"

He looked like I'd just punched him in the face. He reeled in his line and then casted out again, and some twisted line stopped the cast in midair. After it plopped into the lake, he said, "I'm not going to let that happen."

"But you don't know," I said. Neither did I. Nor anyone else, for that matter. "Why do you have to go?" I stopped reeling in my line and just sat there staring out at the lake, deflated.

"I joined the Army to protect you, Abbie. To protect your mother and to protect other families."

"But why you?" Oh, crap. Now it sounded like I was starting to whine. I hate whining.

"Because I'm good at it." What? Because you're good at war? He must have seen the puzzlement in my face. "See, if those of us who are good soldiers stay home, and we send people who can't cut it, then no one is safe. Not anywhere. So I have to go."

Silence. I don't want to ask any more, know any more. I'm a pragmatist, though, so I focused on the details. "Will we have to move?"

"No, honey. Not this time. You and Mom will stay right here until I get home." He pulled in his line, cast it another time. "Is that what worries you?"

"Sometimes. We moved a lot. I'd like to stay here for a while. But I'd move if I could still be with you."

"I'll stay in touch as much as I can. We can email and write and talk. Maybe not all the time, but when I can." He thought for a minute. "You're my princess, and your king might have to go to battle to protect his people. I'll return and we will live happily ever after."

"I thought you were a knight..."

"You got me," he replied. Just then, my rod started to pull and we both jumped into action. "You got one!"

I frantically started to reel in the fish. Anything but continue this conversation. A 19-inch bass! There were some joggers passing by as I pulled in out of the lake, cheering that it must be the biggest fish in all of Lake Pflugerville. I wasn't about to correct them.

fter we got home, we brought the fish into the kitchen. I grabbed a fillet knife and started sharpening. Believe me, you don't want to gut a fish with a dull knife. Dad took some newspapers and covered the counter where we would clean them, and filled a bowl with icy water for the upcoming fillets. I snatched one of the fish and started washing off the slime when Mom walked in, wearing her stink face. "How did it go?" she asked, leering down at the carnage.

"Great," said Dad. "She's a smart one, that Abigail." He cut one of the fish from gill to gill, leaving the center bones intact.

"Of course I am," I replied. "Who do you think I get it from?"

"Clearly me."

Mom grunted at this. "Huh."

"You want to give a hand here?"

"Nope. You know the rules. You catch, you clean. I'll cook the fillets, but no fish guts." She pulled some ice out of the freezer and plunked the cubes into her glass.

I made about a one-inch slit in the center back of my fish, holding its head with my other hand, and cut towards the tail. I concentrated on missing the stomach, as even I find that gross. It's not a big deal, just messy and you can wash it out, but yuck.

Mom wasn't done talking about me. Like I wasn't even in the room. "So, how did she take it?"

"I don't know, really. Why don't you ask her?" He peeled off the skin on one side of his fish. "It's kind of hard to explain."

"What, that her father might go to war and never come back?"

Dad froze.

I dropped my finished fillet into the cold-water bowl. "Mom, that's not really helpful."

"Abbie, he is going. We have to be pragmatic and have a plan on how to handle all this change." Dad decided at that moment to put his arms around Mom, but he was all stinky-fish and she brushed him off. He put his arms behind his back and kissed her, a tiny peck on the tip of her perfect nose.

"We knew this could always happen. You're right; we should prepare." He turned back to his fish. "I just want to make it as easy on this family as possible."

"I know." It felt like a balloon of tension between them had popped. I was glad; I had enough to think about right now. I grabbed another fish and stabbed it right in the eye.

～◡◡〜

About a week later, I came home from school and walked into the living room. Now, before I get into any details here, I have to explain something in case you haven't caught onto it yet. You see, my parents were very much in love.

I know, you've figured that out already. Or at least like they act like they're in love. But it was really true. You'd think that would be a good thing, and most of the time I'd agree with you. Except have you ever been out with two friends that were a couple, and they were all into each other? And there you are, watching them make googly eyes and smoochy faces, and you'd much rather be binge-watching tedious old TV Land series like *The Flying Nun* or anything else at that moment? I felt that way a lot.

Some only children have over-protective parents, but mine weren't bad. They let me do most everything that I wanted. And without other kids to practice on, they didn't have much of a clue about what was appropriate for me. I've used that plenty of times to convince them of dubious pursuits, like "I'm the only kid that hasn't seen any *Saw* movies yet!" Or, "Sure, all the kids hang from six-story ledges."

Sometimes, though, it's not a good thing, being the only child. Especially when they're so into each other. Like I'm interrupting their love.

When I walked into the living room, I was surprised to see Dad home from work early. Mom was sitting on the edge of the couch and he was kneeling in front of her, the top of his head on her chest. *Uh-*

oh. Should I disappear? I took one step back, still facing them. I wasn't sure what to do with myself. Then I noticed that Mom was crying. Crap.

My dad turned his head toward me, and I was invisible no more. He reached out with one hand and I moved toward him. I wasn't ready to join their embrace, though. I looked down at the coffee table, trying to figure out what was going on.

Ah. Deployment orders.

I felt like they'd have been better off without me just then. They were in their own bubble, trying to love each other through this nasty news, and I had interrupted them—again. If I had brothers or sisters I could have talked with them, but no, just me alone and the two of them as one.

Being an only child can't be that bad, right? Jesus was an only child.

6

e sat in an auditorium filled with other military families, all facing the same fate, trying to make light of the situation by joking around and laughing. A woman, older than my mom but not by much, approached the podium. Her dark hair had silver streaks and she had a lived-in face, and she had a brightness in her eyes and a lopsided grin.

When she started speaking, her voice was strong, with an artificial cheerfulness that would have been great on a cooking competition show. Not so good with this crowd. We were all trained bullshit-spotters with a preference for straight shooting.

"Good evening everyone. I'm so glad you all could make it. I'm Lauren Reading, battalion Family Readiness Group leader. I'm sure over the next year or so we will all become very familiar with one another."

The crowd in the auditorium listened with stone faces distracted with thoughts of deployment, generally considered a less-than-cheerful prospect. Some looked down, some looked up at the stage with disdain.

She continued, "Scott and I wanted to take this opportunity to talk about how the FRG can assist you in the transition of your soldier's deployment. This is one of many meetings that will help you understand the process before deployment, and what help is available during deployment. We will also prepare you for the exiting time for when your soldiers come home!"

Ugh. Her delivery was not winning over the crowd. It was like Vanna White at a funeral. My dad saw Mom squirming and offered his hand, trying to set her at ease. I love how he's the one going to war, and he's busy making her feel better about it. He raised her hand up, kissing it. They shared an uneasy glance. I just sat there. One of many meetings? Maybe I could get sick or something.

"Now, it gives me pleasure to introduce my husband—and battalion commander—Lieutenant Colonel Scott Reading." The officer, with his salt-and-pepper buzz cut, stood and approached the podium. He looked around the room like he owned it, with a solid understanding of the mood in the room.

"Good evening, everyone. Like my wife pointed out, this is an informational meeting to highlight what the FRG is for and how it can help. Let's make no mistake about this. This is going to be difficult. Your country has asked you, as families, to make a hard and challenging sacrifice in sending your soldiers to war. Your strength as families will be tested and pushed to the limits.

"We all long for words of comfort, where lines of battle cannot be drawn, or promises made. No brilliant words of mine can ease that uncertainty. All I can say is that the leadership that trained them is the same leadership that is dedicated to their safe return. Lauren and I want everyone here to know that we are here to support you and to help you when those times become too much to handle. The support you families show will resonate with your soldiers downrange, and help to give them the strength they will need to accomplish the mission and come back home to you. In times like this, we ask that we all come together as unit and an extended family to support each other. We will all need it. Thank you, and enjoy the evening."

His confident tone grabbed the attention of the audience, but his serious words didn't lighten the mood. As he left the podium, Lauren made her way back. "OK, so with that, we have several tables set up with informational handouts for you to take home as well as drinks and refreshments. Please take this opportunity to get to know those you may not know. It is very important to grow our family and support network. Thank you all for coming."

Before she was even done speaking, the crowd started to shuffle around and rise. They made their way to tables and started picking up brochures. Damion Rodriguez walked up to us.

"Hey," he said to my dad. "Rachel and I were thinking about doing a squad barbecue. We figured that would be better than mandatory fun."

"You mean you don't want to stand around awkwardly making idol conversation with officers who don't want to be there anymore than us?" Dad replied. "Yeah, man. You can count us in. I have a feeling our daughters will be seeing a lot of each other soon anyway. How did Rachel and Megan take it?"

"Megan disappeared to her room for the rest of the night," said Damion. "Rachel handled it better than expected, but she was an Army brat, so she saw it coming."

"Yeah, so did we." He looked down at me and smiled.

Mom turned to Dad. "You ready to get out of here?" she asked.

"Took the words right out of my mouth."

Damion said, "I'm going to find Rachel and do the same. Remember, barbecue, our place, next Friday. Your turn to bring the cheap beer."

"Yeah, man. See you tomorrow." The two shook and fist pumped as they turned in opposite directions. Dad put his arm around my mom as we walked away.

"Anything exciting?" he asked her, looking around at the tables.

"What's not exciting about Army handouts?"

On the day of the barbecue, I took a shower and put on a light peach summer dress. I went down to the kitchen and grabbed our contributions to the pot luck: Corn on the cob with jalapeno-lime aioli for the grill, and watermelon salad with feta and mint. Mom and I both wanted to bring something other than the standard potato salad or coleslaw.

"Abbie, you look great," Mom said as she tried to hug me with my hands full of foodie-foo-foo. It just felt awkward. She washed her hands in the sink and then leaned against the island, drying her hands with an orange-striped kitchen towel.

"There's a couple of beautiful women," Dad said, and with his back to me, he smooched Mom. One beautiful woman and one girl with her hands full of corn and sundries. Not so beautiful as all that.

We piled into the car and headed towards the Rodriguez' house. By the time we arrived, Damion had the barbecue set up and the action was getting started. Damion was Megan's dad and a nice enough guy, although I didn't really know him. *I should be nice to him*, I thought, as he might be the key to my ability to attend summer camp with Megan.

"Meat smells great," my dad called out to Damion, waving at the rest of the eight-man-squad-plus-families.

"Damn right it does!" he shouted back over the noise of all the kids. Most of them were little squealers, running like they were being herded by sheepdogs. He handed off his apron and barbecue tongs to another guy I didn't know and grabbed my dad.

Damion and my dad hustled to set up a game of cornhole, each trying to toss their bag while holding a Shiner Bock bottle in the other hand. They had their usual argument over who got to toss first. The rule is "the ugliest one starts" but this regulation resulted in a long-winded argument over who was most horrible-looking, with a lot of input from the crowd. Damion lost, or won depending on how you look at it. He was judged the ugliest (no contest in my opinion) so he won the right to start the game.

He spun his bag like a pancake, ending up with a boarder. That'd be worth a point if it stayed on the wood until the end of the round. Dad followed up with a high, lofty toss that had a bit of backspin, knocking Damion's boarder off the wood. Then his bag slid into the hole. Corn in the hole! That's three points for Gryffindor.

Two other soldiers, all dressed in civies, stood at the other end of the backyard, under a big live oak tree. "Why on earth are we going to Iraq?" one asked.

"For the fishing!" the other replied. They seemed to find this quip hysterical.

Megan's mom Rachel, my mom, and a few other women sat at the patio table laughing about something, one of them halfway reaching into a baby stroller.

"You know, the good news is that we won't have to deal with boot stench and uniform parts scattered throughout the house," said Rachel.

The women laughed in agreement. "I swear, sometimes I feel like I have another son instead of a husband." Chuckles. None of this banter seemed remotely funny to me.

My mom felt the same way. "I just don't see how you can be so...I don't know...light-hearted about their deployment."

"You just get used to it," Rachel replied. "You have to find the humor in it all. Seems to work for them." She nodded towards the guys, playing games, drinking, and being funny only to themselves.

"I'm not ready for this. It seems like they're happy about going," said Mom.

"Well, what would you expect? It's what they signed up for."

"It's not what I signed up for." Me either, Mom.

"Girl, you can't show him that," replied Rachel. "That's the last thing he needs. He needs you to be proud of him."

"I am proud. Doesn't mean I'm happy about it."

"You think I am?" Rachel scoffed. "Please. This just ain't my first rodeo. She paused. "Wasn't your father in Vietnam?"

"Yes, but I was born after." Mom just looked on as they continue to play and cut up.

I grabbed Megan, the only other person there remotely close to me in age, and we went over and sat on the Rodriguez' play fort where we could see everything. I had my craft bag and pulled out my current project. I was weaving together some colored strings into braids, and wanted a distraction.

I looked up at Megan. "Are you scared?"

"Yeah. Are you?"

"Yeah. I had a nightmare that he never came home."

"I wish they didn't have to go." Megan noticed what I was doing and asked, "What are you making?"

"A friendship bracelet. For him to wear and think of me every day. Do you want to make your dad one? I'll show you how."

I've been making friendship bracelets for like forever, but lately I've been stepping up my game. I'd decided to make the one for my dad extra-special. I have these tiny Miyuki seed beads, and they're fitsy to work with, very pretty without being gaudy, and I thought if the bracelet was thin enough, maybe Dad would actually keep it on his wrist. He's not really a bangle-wearer.

To make it perfect, I decided to use the beads to spell out something special in Morse Code. It would be secret between us. These beads come in every single color I've ever seen, and they're round and perfectly uniform. I thought they'd be great for my code project.

I had to use a wire beading needle along with the braiding of the cords because the beads are so small. You need to string the beads on some embroidery floss. I showed Megan what I was doing, and she started to get interested. "What message should I code?"

"I don't know. Something special between you and your dad, I guess." She scrunched her brow and looked down at the crafting stuff. "Just keep it short;

Morse Code can get kind of long." I showed her the Morse Code translator website on my phone where you can type in any message and get what the code should be. She typed in a few things, trying it out.

I used blue for the basic color of the bracelet, and then chose red for the dots, white for the dashes, and spacers of gold beads. I started on my message: "-.-. -
-- -- . / .... --- -- . / .... .- ..-. ."

Come home safe.

"Did you ask about summer camp?" Megan asked, looking up at me.

"Yeah," I said. "They said they would talk to your parents about it, but I don't think they have."

"Well, with all that's happening, I don't think you'll be going anywhere this summer with your family. I bet they'll be OK with it."

"Yeah, you're right. On the other hand, I'm not sure Mom would want to be alone in the big house, you know? Especially now," I said, staring over at Dad. "Have you decided on your bracelet message yet?"

"I think so." She pointed down at her design: ".. / .-
.. --- ...- . / -.-- --- ..-"

I love you.

~᠇~᠊~

Dad and I decided to go back to Lake Pflugerville one more time before he left. We sat on the Pier Three, just looking out over the water. No fishing this time.

I didn't know what to think or feel. I don't know if it would have been better to know a year in advance or to find out on the day he left. This in-between time was the worst. I worried about him. Did that make me a horrible person, considering that he was serving our country and all sorts of families like ours? Did it make me selfish to think that he valued all those other families more than he valued ours?

"I made you something, Daddy."

He looked down at me, surprised that I had interrupted the silence. "Oh, yeah? What's that?"

"Nothing much. It's just a friendship bracelet." I didn't mention the Morse Code. He could figure that out on his own. Or not. Maybe he'd make the effort; maybe it wouldn't matter to him.

"Just a friendship bracelet?" he asked. "It's so much more than that, baby girl." He slipped it on his wrist.

"I have one, too. Same colors." I showed him my wrist, and he moved his arm to where our wrists were side by side. Mine said, ".-. . -- . -- -... . .-. / -- ." Remember me.

"Now every time you look at it, you'll think of me."

"I'll think of you every day regardless, Abbie. This is just perfect. I love it." He kissed her on the forehead. "Thank you so much. I'll never take it off."

"Promise?"

"Promise."

Abbie looked thoughtful. "One more thing."

"Anything, Cheese Weasel." Seriously? Cheese Weasel? Sheesh.

"Promise you'll come back?"

He hesitated. "I promise."

I held out my hand with the bracelet. "Pinky promise?"

He didn't put his hand up. "Ah, Fair Maiden, with your bracelet of protection how can I come to harm? You have made me bulletproof!"

"Dad." I glared at him. "This isn't a game. You can't magically make everything fine this time, you know. This is real."

"OK, for serious. You know I'll do everything I can to come back to you, no matter what happens to me. But I have a duty."

He had other duties, duties here with us. Is he a soldier or a father? And he didn't pinky promise.

Time to say what I had to say. "I know, Dad. But this is too hard. As of right now, you are gone to me. I can't stand this waiting any more. So I'm saying good-bye right here, at the lake."

I hated the hurt look on his face. But I had to finish this up. "I'm not sad. I have something that the military doesn't have, you see. In my heart, only I know the real you, Daddy. Only I get to see that special smile you do, or when you climb my bedroom wall with me, or how you make me feel perfectly beautiful when I know I really do look like a cheese weasel.

"Other families are more important to you than this one. No worries; I understand. But I have to survive this. In my heart, you're already gone."

I stood up and started walking. I'd walk home no matter what obstacles were in my way. From now on, I would make my own decisions and live my own life. The real ones, you know. How to survive.

7

My folks had gone to the battalion pre-deployment official speechification and parade and more hot dogs and hamburgers and I didn't go. I had said my goodbye and I had meant it. I thought I'd go completely nuts if I had to sit through more band music, more speeches about how brave we all were, more families pretending to be happy while their hearts were being crushed.

I could see the soldiers in my mind, all standing and saluting during the National Anthem. I could hear Miss Vanna Perfect Attitude smiling with her voice but not her eyes and the battalion commander giving yet another speech about how great we are. Papers would be shuffled, throats would be cleared, but no tears would fall. Goes against the code.

Goodbye, Dad.

I stayed splayed on my bed, not sleeping. It was three a.m. but sleep wasn't coming. I made a promise to myself to run and workout harder tomorrow so I'd be exhausted by bedtime. Too tired to worry or feel sorry for myself.

I knew Mom and Dad were still up, too, waiting. Mom wasn't crying, of course. Not in front of Dad. That would be for me, later.

I heard the click of the bedside light come on in their bedroom, next to mine. I could hear my Dad get up. He'd be putting on his uniform now, laid out all perfect. He'd lace up his boots, and blouse his pant legs. I heard murmurings as they said what had to be said.

I heard Dad leave their room and close the door, and I quickly closed my eyes and moved into a sleeping pose. He crept in and stood over me. I didn't move a muscle, didn't breathe. My back was to him just for insurance.

He bent down, gently kissed the top of my head, and whispered, "I love you."

As he rose to leave, I lay there in silence. He walked away, down the stairs, and out the front door. I heard him get into his truck and start the engine.

As the truck pulled off, a small noise reached me from their bedroom. There is goes; now Mom can cry. Good for her.

Maybe not so good for me.

The next morning, the sun was peeking in through the windows as Mom and I came down for breakfast. Our yogurt-and-granola bowls added some crunch to the proceedings, but they weren't good conversationalists. I grabbed my bag and headed off for school. I have no idea where Mom went.

I remember getting to school, and greeting my friends. I remember walking down the hallway booming with shouting and squealing, like every other day.

I sat with my class, listening to Ms. Jean. Apparently, the United States had lifted economic sanctions imposed on Libya 18 years ago, as some kind of reward for its cooperation in eliminating weapons of mass destruction. I so couldn't care. Libya was far from

Texas and far from where my Dad was heading, so it made little difference to me. I was exhausted and my head started the sleep-bobble-wake-jerk dance. The classroom noise sounded like it was coming through a cotton quilt.

Ms. Jean, echoed and distant, said, "Abbie?" She waited for a response and sighed. "Abbie?" The second call of my name was clearer, and at this, I snapped out of my daze and looked at her. The rest of the classroom giggled. Giggled? I hate being surrounded by children.

I don't know how long it went on, but eventually the bell rang for the end of class and I glued my body and mind together, and dragged myself out of the chair.

All at once, everything crashed down. I went to the bathroom and locked myself in a stall, just panicked.

I skipped the rest of my classes and walked towards home, cutting across yards and lots like always. I wasn't heading in a straight line today, though. I wasn't at all anxious to get home. I came across this huge sand hill, so I climbed to the top to see what I might find. I surprised an armadillo that must have dug down into the sand, and he surprised me right back. Someone else must have been here before; there was an old fire pit. Texans will barbecue anywhere.

This new place was silent. The sky was huge and bright blue. I stood there, right at the top of the mound, and started screaming at the top of my lungs. I was screaming so that whatever happened, nothing would hurt me. I was screaming for power. I could feel it coming up through the earth and the sand and the ashes and the armadillo and up through my body and out my mouth.

Finally I must have made it home. That part is still a blur. I was untouchable, even by memory.

I walked through the kitchen, empty except for a shot glass still smelling of booze. Guess Mom is home. I stumbled up to my room, because if you want to lose yourself, the internet is always there for you.

I don't know what to do. But I can always *Ask Jeeves*.

The days passed. Each one a day closer to Dad coming home. I came home from school, walking up to the front door with purpose. I wanted to get inside and barricade myself from the rest of the world. I unlocked and forced open the door, entered and shut it behind me. I leaned back against the door, feeling like now I could let go. I slid down until I was sitting on the foyer's Spanish tile floor, let a few tears fall. *Breathe, Abbie,* I told myself, and got my brain-monkeys corralled into their containment barrel.

I stood up and went to the kitchen, and Mom. And nagging. "I'm not going to constantly remind you to take out the garbage."

"I'm sorry. Dad usually does it." And he should be here, doing it, not me.

"Well, he's not here, is he?" said Mom. "It may not seem like a big deal to you, but I need these things done."

"I'm sorry."

"I don't need you to be sorry. I need you to be responsible."

And I don't give a crap what you need. Always you; never me. I'm gone.

"Don't walk away from me!" my mom shouted. "Abbie?" she asked, softer.

Mom was close to losing it, too. I was sorry about that but she was supposed to be the grownup. I was already lost. If I didn't find myself, how on earth could I fill her deep pit of need? It just kept growing.

8

egan and I hung out in their back yard. Mom and I had come over for a visit, and it wasn't going very well. My mom sat, lost in thought. Rachel called her name, snapping her out of it. They sat by a fire pit on the back porch. We were nearby, but I think they thought we were somewhere else, or else we didn't much matter.

Mom had a glass of wine in her hand.

"You awake over there?" asked Rachel, Megan's mom.

"Sorry. Just zoned out."

"You're killing yourself. You know that, right?"

"What do you mean?"

"Worrying like you are."

"How could I not?" Mom sipped some wine. "Don't act like you're not."

"You kidding? I worry every day. I just don't let it run my life."

"Well, the news doesn't help when..."

Rachel interrupted. "That's your first problem, you need to stop watching that crap. Doom and gloom. You'll never hear anything good."

"Yeah, you're right."

"How's Abbie handling it?"

"Not well. I'm hoping this Orienteering Club helps. She needs a distraction." Mom looked back to the fire pit and stared.

~∿~

There were 11 students that had decided to sign up for Orienteering Club. Orienteering is basically running through the bush using a map and compass to try and find the fastest way somewhere. It's kind of opposite to parkour, and yet complementary at the same time. In parkour, you find the shortest route. In orienteering, you find the fastest route. Sometimes they're the same, but often they're not. I like knowing both ways. I sat with Megan, although I was pretty zoned out.

Megan looked pretty good, all prepared with green cargo pants, a long-sleeved shirt that was red with a tiger-stripe pattern in black, walking boots, and hair pulled back under a Diamondbacks ball cap. Megan always had a way of making the truly bizarre something cool. She wasn't always that way. She had her my-little-pony rainbow dolphin horse phase like a lot of the girls did, but that was ago. Now she was devil-may-care cool.

Our school counselor led the Orienteering Club. He was a pretty good-looking guy for a grown up, with silver hair and darker eyebrows. He had blue eyes and a pleasant face, kind of like someone who rescued dogs or landed a plane safely in an emergency. He introduced himself as Christopher Long, but we could call him, "Mr. Chris." Decent enough.

Orienteering is a lot of fun, usually. I was kind of in a mood, though, so I wasn't as into it as I usually am. You have to find markers, called controls. You can only carry a compass, a map with the controls marked, and a whistle. That's so if you run into trouble or get lost or something, you can blow on it and hope someone smarter shows up.

I don't think there's anyone smarter than me, so I don't ever use the whistle.

Orienteers notice stuff. And they're problem-solvers. I like having those skills. Plus you get to run a lot. It's like cross-country but you get to make your own route.

"Today we're going to focus on fog training. I'm going to give you a map with most of the course removed. Some circles of the map are still there, but the between parts are gone—like they're fogged out—and so you have to use your compass to get between the detailed areas that are left," explained Mr. Chris. "It's good training in compass use, and you have to use details that you wouldn't use normally in orienteering. I want you to run the course in pairs, and check each other's compass and map work."

Megan and I teamed up, naturally. We both like orienteering. It's kind of good leadership mojo, too, too—you need to have bearing, to have goals, to know where you want to go. If you don't know where you're going, how will you know when you get there? I think good leadership is like good orienteering. Make sure you have the right map for the ground you are on, acquire and use the necessary equipment correctly to orienteer your way most efficiently and effectively through the course, and be quicker than your competitors to win the race.

We warmed up as a group, then got into our pairs. Megan and I looked over the map together, plotting how we wanted to take the course. The fastest route today didn't seem be the shortest, so we decided to aim off, heading for a trail that ran parallel to the control. Once we found and hit the trail, it would be simple and fast to turn and hit the target. Then we cleared our finger sticks that track us on the route and times us. We each inserted our finger stick into the start unit to start the course, and we were off.

We started running in our chosen direction. It was peaceful out here, and the running was hypnotic. Our hard breathing made conversation difficult, so we just ran together in silence.

My mind wandered as my feet did their stuff.

I wished I could fly, fly away just as fast as I was running, my feet plopped firmly to the ground with each stride. Gravity. No flight, just running, jumping over branches, vaulting over boulders.

The darkness of the forest pressed in all around me while my body screamed for faster and faster speeds. The decomposing leaves smelled like anger and loss.

As I ran, my heart started pounding hard. I felt like I was looking down a tunnel, and my hands started tingling. Something was wrong. I was going to die, right here. I couldn't see Megan anywhere in my tunnel as I ran and ran. There was no one who would come for me. Dad was gone, Mom was probably drunk, I was lost somewhere and didn't know what to do. I had completely forgotten the club and the course—I just ran for my life.

I heard a sound, very quiet, along with the bam, bam, bam of my feet. A little tweet. Then louder. Someone was blowing a whistle. My whistle. I could blow it and someone would come.

I fell to my knees and put the whistle in my mouth, blowing it over and over. I slammed my palm on the ground to keep the rhythm going—bam, bam, bam. It helped. Tweet and bam.

After forever, I felt someone's hands on my shoulders, pulling me up. I went limp, the whistle falling from my mouth to the ground. My vision focused—Mr. Chris was looking at me, worried. My vision expanded. All the other kids were standing there, staring at me. No one seemed to know what to do.

Mr. Chris took control, and that helped. He said, "It's important to have strength in your body to be successful at orienteering. We also have to be strong in our minds and our hearts. Abbie's just shown us a great lesson. When there's trouble, we reach out to each other and help. Everyone here came to be strong with her. Well done." I breathed deeper, slower. "Good job, Abbie. Let's all walk back and finish today's lesson."

We headed back. He talked quietly to me, explaining about panic attacks, and that I shouldn't worry, they were pretty common and I wasn't going to die. I felt ridiculous. But I was alive, and that was good enough for right now.

⌒﹏﹏⌒

Mom drove me home from the club meeting as I sat in the back seat staring aimlessly out the window. She looked back at her through the rearview mirror, but was silent, like she didn't know what to say. Finally, she spoke. "I was thinking we should stop for some dinner. You have anything in mind?"

I didn't break my gaze out the window. "I'm not hungry."

9

ad wasn't feeling the emptiness like we were. He was busy, I'm sure, fighting the war and leading his soldiers.

You're probably wondering what it's like over there, so let's see if I can make it real for you, like it was for my dad. Start by finding the vacuum cleaner. Pop that sucker open and grab the dust bag. OK, now pour that over your head. Get it good in your nose and eyes. Hit yourself in the chest and make sure that you cough up a good cloud. It's a start.

I'm sure you think it's hot, and yeah, that's true, during the day. At night try walking over a frozen rock garden. Fun, no? You have to walk over that to get to the bathroom in the dark. And the during-the-day-hot isn't like a warm summer day, even here in Texas. Think living inside a blow dryer. On high. While wearing a suit of armor. We're getting closer.

Oh, yeah, and while all that is going on, people are trying to kill you. While you are breaking into their houses.

My dad told me that he was wearing that bracelet I gave him one balmy summer day as he held his weapon. He and his squad were clearing rooms in what remained of an apartment complex. He could hear thumps as doors were kicked open; random voices calling, "Clear."

He did the same. Just another door, just another room. Everything got loud and bright and white. Ears ringing as he lay on the floor staring at the ceiling. It was covered with a torn fabric decoration—of *Lilo and Stitch*. Real? Hallucination?

Rodriguez bent down, dragging Dad back out of the room, leaning towards his face trying to get his attention. He slapped him a couple of times. Why not?

My dad shook himself, coming back to reality.

"Thought I lost you there, brother," said Rodriguez, smiling.

Dad was still shaking but smiled back, still on the alert. Was there still a threat? He had to be on alert all the time, for himself and for the rest of the group. He crawled a little bit, and then asked, "We done yet?"

"Not even close."

"Then let's get to it."

Rodriguez reached out to give him a hand up. Dad weighed a lot more than usual with all that gear. Time to kick the next door. Good thing he wasn't alone. Rodriguez would always have his back. Dad believed in people.

10

In my dream, I was walking home but somehow, I couldn't find it. I knew the area I was in, and everything looked familiar, but I turned the wrong way and then I couldn't find the right street again. I was so terrified. I thought I woke up, but I couldn't seem to move a single muscle. Something strange was happening. Something evil.

It was a ghost oppression, a dead body that landed on my chest. The emotion of my dream flooded over me. There was something awful in the room with me and I couldn't see what it was.

A shriek poured out of my mouth. I heard my door open and my mom was there, rushing to me, onto my bed, pulling me into her arms. She held me until the shaking stopped. We stayed there until I drifted off, exhausted.

It was only a light doze this time, though. I heard her leave the room and go back to her bed. She was talking. She had called someone.

I heard, "She's never done this before." A pause. "I just don't know what to do. She seems to be getting worse. She's not crazy; she's just scared. Aaron being gone had really messed with her." Pause. "I know. Do you think you could come, even just for a week? I think you visiting would really help." Pause. "OK, OK. I love you, too."

Who was coming? Then I drifted off again.

The next morning, I went down for breakfast and Mom was at the table reading the paper, looking worried. I opened the refrigerator to get some juice. The light flickered, and then a clunking whirr. Lights out.

Mom went to look behind the fridge to check if it was plugged in—yes.

Dead as a doornail.

We looked at each other and both burst into tears.

～ა～ა～

The doorbell rang. Mom went to answer it, and with curiosity getting the better of me, I crept to see who was at the door. Mom opened the door revealing Grandpa Tom holding a small suitcase. I lept up to greet him.

"Grandpa!" I shouted, then ran and jumped into his arms.

"Ooph," said Grandpa as he tried to pick me up. "Hey there! You're almost getting to big for that!"

"How long are you staying?" I asked.

"A few days, sweetie." He held me at arm's length and looked at me. "Look at you! Your mom better watch out. You took every bit of pretty from her!"

"Very funny," said Mom. Funny? Why don't you think I'm pretty, Mom?

She moved to hug her father and kissed him on the cheek, whispering in his ear. "Thanks for coming."

He came in and she shut the door behind him.

That night, I lay in bed, with Grandpa right beside me.

"You get some sleep, now." He leaned forward to kiss me on the forehead. I caught him right before he stood back up.

"Grandpa?"

"Yes?" he replied.

"Is Mom OK?"

"Of course she is. Why wouldn't she be?"

"She just doesn't seem happy." Understatement of the world.

Grandpa thought for a minute. "Well, it's not a very easy time for any of us, but she'll be fine. As will you." He offered me a warm smile. I only returned half of one.

"What are you basing that on? How can you know she'll be fine? Please don't just feed me a line. It doesn't make my fear go away, you know."

"I know, little one. But don't you worry that pretty head of yours. Time is going go by and he'll be back before you know it." Ugh. More pointless words that don't address the problem or treat me like I can think for myself. Adults never seem to get that telling us not to worry doesn't make us not worry. It just makes us lie to them. Grandpa continued, repeating himself, "Now, don't you worry and get to sleep."

"Yes, Grandpa." Please go.

He reached over to the lamp, turning it off, then left my room, gently pulling the door closed.

He walked down the stairs, and after a few minutes, I crept out of my room to listed to the adults talk. Maybe I could actually learn something of substance.

Grandpa and Mom were in the kitchen. The door stood open. I didn't move a muscle.

"Can I get you a drink?" asked Mom.

"You know I quit that stuff. And from the looks of it, you should, too."

Mom wasn't happy with that response. "Novel, coming from you."

"You called me here. I came to help the two of you, not to fight about my past. I will, however, call it how I see it." He paused for a minute. "You don't think I know how this goes? How it ends? I've seen that face looking back at me in the mirror before. Have you looked in the mirror lately?"

"I don't need a lecture from you. I'm...."

Grandpa interrupted her. "Yes, you do, and you're going to listen." His voice grew louder, which was good for me, but probably just pissed of Mom more. "That wonderful little girl up there needs you, and you've checked out. Her father can't be here, but you can. I will not sit back and let do to her what I did to you."

"Dad, it's not the same," said Mom.

"Every case is different, and every case is exactly the same. The cycle has to end, and it needs to end with you. You've got a good man and an amazing child. Do not throw it all away."

"And what if Aaron doesn't..." She struggled to get the rest out, started to choke on her words, and fought not to cry.

"You can't allow yourself to think like that. The only way she's going to get better is if you are strong. And you're not going to find that strength at the bottom of that." He must have meant the bottles of booze that were sucking the life out of my mother.

She didn't answer for a moment. "The fridge is broken." Changing the subject. She was great at deflecting any conversation she didn't like.

Grandpa sighed, probably resigned to not having gotten through to her. "I'll give it a look."

An empty kitchen. Silence. Ring. The phone started to blink. Footsteps pattered into the kitchen. I crossed over to answer the phone.

"Hello?" I listened for the response, my heart beating too hard. "Daddy!" I mashed the button to put him on speaker and then sat down at the counter.

"How ya doin', baby girl?"

"OK, I guess."

"You guess? What's going on? Where's your mother?" Dad asked. Ah.

"She's sleeping."

"At this hour?"

"Do you want me to wake her?"

"No; it's fine, sweetie," he answered. "You can just tell her I called, and that I love her. But what's going on with you?"

"I just really miss you, Dad."

"I miss you, too. Mom says you're seeing a counselor now. How is that going?"

"It's going good. I really like him."

"That's great, Cheese Weasel. I really hate that I'm not there."

"I really hate that, too." I looked down at my wrist, running my fingers over the woven cord and beads. "You still have your bracelet?"

"Of course I do, Abbie. It never comes off." I smiled. Then Grandpa walked through the kitchen entryway and leaned against the door frame. I looked up, raised my eyebrows in a silent do-you-want-to-talk motion. He shook his head. Just going to listen, I guess.

"Look, if you could tell your mother that it might be a few days before I can call back. A little bit longer than normal."

"I can do that."

"Thank you, sweetie. It's time for me to go. I love you so much. Kisses to you and your mother."

"Kisses back, Dad. I love you, too."

"Bye, Abbie." I hung up, sitting in silence, and then I went over to Grandpa and we both went into the living room. The off-white living room. Could it kill Mom to put some color in this house? It was all so beige. My feelings were jumbled up and my stomach hurt. I curled into Grandpa's lap with a frustrated sigh.

"Grandpa?"

"Mmm?"

"What was it like?"

He knew what I meant. Grandpa never did need long explanations to understand me. He sat back and said, "Your mother asked me that same question when she was about your age. I tell you, it isn't any easier to answer now than it was then." He looked like he was trying to figure out the best angle for my tender years. That wasn't going to cut it with me.

"I want to know what Dad's going through. Please. Tell me."

"Well, it's scary," he began. "I know you probably understand at least that, but it's not like what you see on the news all the time."

Grandpa drifted into his own memories. "There's mostly a lot of waiting around. A lot of boredom. And sudden craziness—then more boredom."

He was going to sanitize it for me. "Did you kill anyone?"

He wasn't expecting that question quite so soon. "I wouldn't worry about that. We all kind of did what we had to." He clearly didn't want to answer the question. And just as clearly, he had answered it. If he hadn't killed anyone, he would have just said so. "I will tell you this," he went on. "You know the men that he's with?"

I nodded. I'd let it go this time and see where Grandpa was going with his explanation.

"Well, I'm sure you've seen how they are around each other."

"Yeah—they're pretty weird."

Tom laughs, seeing his way out of the conversation. "Well, that weirdness, as you put it, is something they have together that keeps them going. It's a kind of love, like loving a brother or sister." I wouldn't know about that. "They look out for and take care of each other. Your father is a leader, but his men respect him and just like he takes care of them, they will do the same." I shifted my weight. "You've nothing to worry about."

Except that I had seen the news and the second battle of Fallujah was right there in my television. They said it was the heaviest urban combat since Vietnam. And the bloodiest.

Glad to know I have nothing to worry about.

11

ack at school, our new teacher, Ms. Ledbetter, called role. There were some new students, too.

"Jeffery Kauffman."

"Here."

"Samantha Block."

"Here."

"Abigail Matthews."

"Here," I replied passively. A couple of seats away sat Krista Morris, that girl who loved to torment me. She was looking back and snickering with some other girls. I looked away. Never make eye contact with a predator.

I swear, there are no well-adjusted students in this school at all. I hate Middle School. It's like someone decided to take the most immature age groups possible and shove them together in some kind of cage match.

Later, the students were all looking down, writing. Except me. I was lost in thought—on another planet. I hadn't written a thing. Ms. Ledbetter took notice.

The bell rang, and we all got up to gather our things and leave this prison. As I walked out, I passed Ms. Ledbetter's desk.

"Abbie?" the teacher asked.

I stopped and faced her. "Yes, Ma'am?"

"Did you have any questions about the assignment?"

"No, Ma'am."

"Are you sure? If you have any questions at all, you can ask. I'm here to help."

"I know." I wanted to leave, and not discuss anything with her. Take a hint.

"OK. Well, you have a good weekend, all right?"

"Yes, Ma'am. You too." I exited smartly, stage left. I didn't look back. I didn't want to see her expression, or any concern or pity.

A few weeks later, there was a Parent/Teacher conference at school. I was doing homework in the dining room when Mom came back. She came in and sat down. I guess she wanted to tell me all about it. I was a lot less interested.

"I talked with Ms. Ledbetter," Mom said, jumping into the briefing.

"OK."

"She thinks you're very sweet." I snorted. Mom went on, "Quiet, too. She asked about Dad."

I looked up. "What about him?"

"If him being deployed had affected you."

"How could it not affect me?"

"Well, of course it would. I think she was trying to find a reason why your grades are slipping."

"Hm."

"I didn't know your grades were slipping. That's not acceptable, Abbie."

"To who?" It's acceptable to me.

"To me. And your dad. You know what he thinks about grades."

"Well, he's not here, and it's not like you've shown any interest."

"I'm interested now." Oh, Mom. Just when I was getting used to your under-parenting, too. "I'm going to pay more attention, and help you with your homework or whatever you need to get your focus back."

"She was wondering if you wanted to be in the school Christmas play."

I looked her right in the eye. "I have no interest in that." I don't want anyone to even notice me. Why would I want the whole school looking at me?

"Well, you like Orienteering Club, right?"

"Yes..."

"If you're grades keep slipping, I don't think you can keep doing after-school stuff."

"Mom!"

"Think about it." She looked at me, like she was seeing me for the first time. "I want our relationship to be solid, Abbie."

"By threatening me?"

"I'm not threatening you. I'm just letting you know that your choices have consequences."

Yeah. So do yours, Mom.

I had a panic attack at school. I didn't realize it until after it was over. We were just sitting at our desks, doing our school work, and it was quiet. Nothing that should have scared me or anything. The paper I was reading started to go fuzzy, and my heart started pounding, and I couldn't catch my breath. I wished that my teacher was Mr. Chris as he seemed to know all about these attacks. I didn't trust Ms. Ledbetter yet. Even though I knew what it was, when I was in the middle of an attack, my brain couldn't think clearly and so I couldn't break myself out of it.

I grabbed the sides of my desk and my eyes teared up. Then I heard a voice saying, "Abbie? Are you OK?" Ms. Ledbetter. Well, we were going to find out if she knew what to do. "Abbie? Look at me, Abbie. Try to focus on me. Breathe, Abbie. It's OK—it's OK."

I started to slow my breathing down and Ms. Ledbetter's voice went from an echo to clear and she came into focus. There. I was back.

"Abbie. Are you OK?" How do you answer that? I had no idea if I was OK.

"Here," Ms. Ledbetter continued. "Why don't we take you to the nurse and give you a minute?" Ms. Ledbetter took my hand and helped her stand. I must have looked like a preschooler. As we began to leave the classroom, we passed by Krista's desk.

"Freak."

I heard it. Didn't react. She was right.

12

fter I left the nurse's office, the bell rung. I squeezed past a group of bigger kids who couldn't care less if they were late for anything. Too cool to hurry, cool enough to block the entire hall. I entered the flow of people, just wanting to make it back to class.

I crossed my arms tightly in front of me to make herself smaller. I wanted to disappear into the crowd.

I looked down at my feet and not where I was going. Dumb. Smack—collision, and I almost fell to the ground. She looked to see who ran into me and there was Krista, looking right back.

"Watch out, freak." She pushed me, knocking my school stuff to the floor. "What, you gonna cry now? Are you a little baby?" I would never give her the satisfaction of tears. I had many things in my life worth crying over. She was most certainly not one of them.

I tried to walk around her, but Krista blocked the attempt.

"Do you want your daddy? Oh, wait, he's gone. Probably dead."

Seriously? OK, now I was just pissed. I popped one right into her smug face, knocking her to the floor. Take that.

Krista lay on the ground while other students gathered around, some cheering for me, others for Krista. I stood over her, daring her to get up and face me.

Ms. Ledbetter entered the hallway at all the shouting and saw Krista on the ground, holding her face and starting to cry. I hovered, threatening.

"Abbie! What is going on here?" Ms. Ledbetter cried.

Krista called out, "Abbie punched me! Out of nowhere! What's the matter with her?"

"You're coming with me, Abbie. We have to see Mr. Thompson." I didn't argue. Back to the offices we go.

My mom stormed into the principal's office, leaving the door open. Mr. Thompson was sitting at his desk. I sat with Ms. Ledbetter across from him. Mr. Thompson stood to greeted my mom—not over-friendly, given the circumstances.

"Mrs. Matthews," he said, shaking her hand. "Pleasure to meet you." He moved behind her and shut the door, then leaned on the front of his desk.

"Mrs. Matthews," he continued. "We had an incident today—rather, more of an altercation with another student. I'll let Ms. Ledbetter explain a little more since she's attached to the situation."

"Earlier today, I sent Abbie to the school nurse, and..."

"Wait, school nurse?" interrupted Mom. "What for?"

"Abbie had a situation in class today. The nurse thinks it was an anxiety attack."

"And why wasn't I called immediately?"

The principal said, "The nurse didn't think it was emergency. Thought she just needed some time to decompress."

Ms. Ledbetter continued, "That's when the altercation happened with another student. According to Abbie, this student bumped her in the hallway and started taunting her. Abbie then struck the student hard enough to knock her to the ground."

Mom said, "Let me get this straight. You call me in here about her dealing with a bully, but don't bother to call me about her having an anxiety attack in the middle of class?"

"Like I said, the nurse didn't feel…"

"I don't care what the nurse thought. I care about being informed about things related about my child's health."

"I understand, Mrs. Matthews, it's just that…

"…that defending herself against a bully is more of a priority."

"That's not what I was going to…" Mr. Thompson stopped to take a breath. "Look, the safety of the students is our number one concern, and our policy against physical violence is a top priority and had to be addressed."

"And what of your policy on bullying? Is this other student being dealt with?"

"We don't discuss disciplinary actions in regards to other students."

"Meaning that you're doing nothing. It's good to know where your priorities are." Mom looked at me, all mama-lion-fierce. Pretty cool. "Come on, Abbie. We're leaving."

We started to go, but before we could leave Mr. Thompson spoke up. "Mrs. Matthews, we're not done addressing this incident."

"I am."

"We are going to suspend Abbie for three days."

"Excuse me? Suspended? My daughter gets abused by this girl, puts an end to it, and you're going to suspend Abbie. Am I missing something here?"

"Our hands are tied," Mr. Thompson said. "We have to act in accordance to current school policy. There is an alternative to suspension, however."

"And that is?"

"If she is enrolled in counseling, it can act in lieu of the suspension. We've done that before and it has proven helpful."

"Abbie does not need counseling," she insisted.

"She's been struggling a great deal lately, and after speaking at length with Ms. Ledbetter and Ms. Jean, we think this outburst was a culmination of things outside of just this other student. Of the only two options, we believe that counseling would be the most beneficial."

"The good news is that the Republic of Texas has provisions for licensed family counselors in schools, and our councilor is terrific. He's helped many children from broken homes," added Ms. Ledbetter. I had to see a shrink? Because our home was broken? I'd rather have been suspended. I could have used a three-day break.

"She's not in a broken home. Her father is just overseas."

"Yes, we understand that, but the reactions are the similar because of the length of the separation. At least consider it. And Abbie already knows him—he runs the Orienteering Club."

Mr. Chris? That might be OK. He was all right. "I could do that, Mom," I said softly.

"Thank you," said Mr. Thompson. "We don't want to suspend Abbie—she's been an exemplary student."

"Well, I hope for the sake of the other students, you do something about the one who isn't." Before either of them had a chance to respond, we made our escape.

We rode home, quiet at first. I broke the silence. "That was pretty cool, Mom, standing up for me like that."

She changed the subject off of her and on to me. "It's getting worse, isn't it?"

"What is?"

"The nightmares, problems at school. You hardly ever talk anymore."

"You don't talk either."

"Abbie, this isn't you," said Mom. "The Abbie I know is sweet, kind and respectful—and wouldn't dream of raising her hand to anybody."

"Maybe you should talk to that Abbie." Since she liked her better than she liked me.

"Abbie! How dare you talk to me like that!"

"It wasn't my fault!"

"That's no excuse. You come talk to me about it so I can handle it."

I looked out the window. "Not like anyone would do anything anyway."

"That's not true."

"Yes, it is. You don't talk to me either. You don't ask me anything. You just drink. You don't care."

It was truth-telling time. "I wish Dad were home."

"I do, too. But he's not."

We both went back to silence. The air in the car was suffocating.

13

om and I sat in a waiting area just outside of an office door with a name plate that read Christopher Long, LMFT. Counselor.

We sat in silence. The door opened and Mr. Chris walked out. He walked over to me, reaching out for a handshake. I stood up to take his hand.

"Hello, Abbie. Great to see you." Mr. Chris looked up at Mom, smiling. "I'm Christopher Long. You must be Stacy. Pleasure to meet you."

"Nice to meet you, Chris," she responded.

"Please, come in and make yourselves comforta-ble." The three of us walked back into the office.

Mr. Chris shut the door behind him as Mom and I took our seats on the couch. The room was cozy and warm. Two couches formed an L-shape in the corner, opposite Chris's desk.

Certificates and filled book shelves adorned the walls. Master's Degree. MS in Marriage & Family Counseling/Therapy from Abilene Christian University.

I was wide-eyed and a bit nervous, but I think I contained it well. Chris sat on the adjoining couch next to them.

Mr. Chris knew I was nervous, and he tried to make me feel more comfortable. "So, Abbie, how has your day been?"

"Good, I guess."

"Well, I want you both to know that I understand that this can be kind of scary, and I don't want you to think that you have any reason to be nervous. This is a safe place and you should know that I am here to help. I generally like to invite the parents in to help put their minds at ease as well, since they can sometimes be more nervous. Abbie already knows me, but in a different capacity. You need to know that whatever happens in here stays here, and won't ever be a part of our Orienteering Club or anything else in school."

Mom simply nodded.

Mr. Chris continued. "As I understand it, your dad is currently deployed overseas. How often are you two able to talk to him?"

Mom replied, "We talk about two or three times a week."

"That's good. Abbie, are you excited when you are able to talk to him?"

"Yeah, I am, but sometimes it makes me miss him more."

"That's completely natural," said Mr. Chris. "How long has he been gone?"

"Almost nine months," said Mom. Mr. Chris kept his eyes on me, I guess to see how I reacted to Mom's response. I kept looking down.

"OK, well, it's no secret that this is a difficult time, but I will help you get through it."

I looked up and gave him a half smile. He stood up and walked over to his desk and picked up a manila folder. "Like all bureaucracies, there's some paper-work to fill out. Stacy, if you could fill this out and give the forms to Abbie to bring in next time we talk, that would be great. When would you like to start, Abbie? Maybe next week?"

"Next week is perfect," said Mom, answering for me.

"OK. I see you have an open period on Wednesdays. Want to spend that time with me instead of in study hall?"

"That's fine."

Even though he was directing the questions to me, I sat quietly. Mom was doing all the answering for me anyway. I didn't really feel a part of what was happening. I really liked Mr. Chris, and he was a great orienteering coach, but this was something different, and I didn't know how it would go. Mr. Chris must have figured out that I wasn't really there. He came over to me and said, "Don't worry, Abbie. Everything's going to be fine. I'll see you next week, OK?"

I just nodded.

⌒‿⌒‿⌒

Megan and I sat on the back patio at Megan's house. I was fidgeting with my bracelet. "So I'm having to talk to this counselor now," I began. "And it's Mr. Chris. How weird is that?"

"Because of the fight with Sara?"

"Yeah. And other stuff."

"She deserved it, said Megan. "She was really mean. She's mean to other girls, too."

"I still feel bad for doing it," I said.

"Don't you like him?"

"Mr. Chris? Sure. I mean, he's nice. But for personal stuff? That's just bizarre. I see him by myself on Wednesday."

"What are y'all gonna talk about?" asked Megan.

"I dunno. Dad being gone, I guess. Aren't you sad about your dad being gone?"

"Yeah, but my mom is used to it. My Papi was in the Army, too, and was gone a lot. So that helps a little." I just looked down at my bracelet.

∼◡◡◠

Mr. Chris and I sat on the couch. He was next to me, with plenty of space between us, but at least we were facing the same direction so I didn't have to look right at him if I didn't want to.

I wasn't in the mood for this. "So you're going to fix me, right?"

He laughed. "No, Abbie. Counseling won't fix you, because you're not broken. I'm just here to help you find strengths that you might not know you have, and to teach you some new skills that might make it easier for you to deal with the challenges you're facing, or might face in the future."

"You're not going to cure me?"

"No, Abbie. You're not sick. My goal is to make sure you have the resources to deal with life, both its good points and crappy ones." That didn't sound too bad.

"So how do we start?"

"Normally, I would ask you a bunch of questions and you would answer. But I don't want to really do that. I just want you to talk."

"About what?"

"About anything you want. You can talk about school, you can talk about things you like, you can talk about your dad, what makes you angry, what makes you happy, what you like doing, even your favorite subject in school. Anything is fair game."

"I dunno, really." I still didn't have any idea how to open up to my coach. "I guess I'm supposed to talk about my dad."

"I don't want you to think that you have to talk about anything specific. If you want to talk about him, please do."

Inside my skull there were so many words scrambling to get out, but my mouth wasn't cooperating. I was afraid if I started talking I wouldn't be able to stop. And then I'd start screaming again. "Well, I miss him a lot. A whole lot." Mr. Chris didn't say anything. He sat there like some serene buddha. He was like a silence that needed filling, pulling the words out of my brain. "He's never been gone this long before. Only a few days sometimes. He calls it being in the field. There was one time he was in California for a month, and I didn't like that, but this is worse." I stopped for a sec, trying to corral the thoughts into something cohesive.

"When he would come back from being gone a few days, he would always stink." I chuckled at the memory. "Mom would always yell at him to go take a shower before he touched her, and he'd chase her around the house trying to hug her.

"I could smell him sometimes too, and he did stink, but it was funny. We would always go out to eat when he got back from stuff like that." I missed doing that. And fishing. "We go fishing a lot. Well, we used to, you know, before he left.

"I didn't like it when he first took me. I agreed with Mom. Fish smell terrible. But I liked spending time with him. Now I love fishing. The smell doesn't bother me anymore and we always have so much fun. We joke around a lot, and sometimes we don't talk, but it's still fun, ya know?

"I always hate it when it ends. I just want to go fishing with him again."

"You know," Mr. Chris finally said, "I am sure those days will come back when he comes back home."

"I hope so."

"Do you and you mother have something like that?"

"She never comes with us because she hates the way fish smell."

"What about something else? Something that only you do with her."

"Not really," I said. "I only come home from school and she takes me back and forth, but we don't really do much together."

"Would you like to?"

"I guess. I'm not sure what we would do."

"I have something I'd like you to do." I looked at him, wondering what he'd assign me. More home-work; joy. Probably about feelings and stuff.

"I want you to write a letter to your Mom."

"What?"

"You don't have to send it or anything. You abso-lutely don't need to have her read it, either, unless you want to. You don't even need to show it to me. It's a way for you to organize your thoughts about her, what maybe you'd like to say to her if you had a chance and if she would listen."

Well, that sounded like something I could do. "Thank you. Should I bring it with me next time?"

"That's up to you. It's your letter. You don't have to show me or anyone unless you choose to." I smiled.

Back in class, I sat at my desk focused on writing. I was thinking about another conversation I had with Mr. Chris.

"How often do you see her drinking?" he had asked.

"A lot more lately. She used to only do it at night, but now I see her doing it during the day and she falls asleep on the couch a lot. Sometimes I can't wake her up to take me to school."

"So how do you get there?"

"I walk."

Back in Mr. Chris' office, I just couldn't keep my hands still. They were like birds in a cage trying to fly away.

He asked, "Does she ever get angry with you for things?"

"Not really. Only when I hit that girl at school. She doesn't talk to me much anymore, and she's always sad."

"Well, I'm sure that she is sad about your father being gone."

I responded, "I know that she is, but it's not like that. I dunno. It's just—a different kind of sadness. I guess that doesn't make sense."

"No, it makes perfect sense. I understand what you mean. She does still love you, though."

"I know, but I wish she would tell me more. I can't remember the last time she said it."

We sat quietly for a few minutes. Then I got my courage up. "Is it OK if I ask you a question?"

"Sure," he answered, surprised.

"You have a lot of pictures here in your office. I don't see any of your family. Is that some kind of therapy thing? Like we're not supposed to know anything about you?"

"No, it's not really that. I'm a school counselor first, and I like having things around the room that make the students, like you, more comfortable. Would you feel better if I had family pictures around?"

"Well, maybe." I thought about it for a minute. "I guess it just feels a little odd talking about my parents and not knowing anything about yours, you know?"

"That's logical. I guess I don't have pictures out because my mom passed away. I do miss her a lot. That's probably why I don't have her picture here."

"What about your Dad?"

"We don't talk much, unfortunately. He really withdrew after my mom died."

"Maybe you should write him a letter."

Mr. Long burst out laughing. "What's good for the goose, huh?"

"If it's good advice for me, maybe it would be for you."

He chuckled again. "Maybe. What I do know is that I wanted to do this job so I could help other families communicate. Is there anything you feel drawn to do, because of your experience?"

"I'd have to think about that."

"OK. We can talk more about that later. You were saying that you wish that your mom would tell you that she loves you more often, right?"

"Yeah. It sounds sort of weak, though. I should be strong enough to not need to hear it, I think."

"What would happen if you walked up to her for no reason and told her that you love her?"

"What?"

"I mean, it's sometimes helpful to turn things around. If it would help you to hear it, it might help her to hear it from you. Do you tell her you love her very often?"

"I don't think I ever say it."

"Well, maybe you could try it once, as an experiment. See what happens."

"What happens when you tell your father you love him?"

He laughed again. "Oh, no, sneaky-pete. No turning the tables. This time is for you to explore new ways of handling your life. I'll talk about my life with my therapist."

"You see a therapist?"

"Sure. Everyone needs a little help clarifying their lives sometimes. OK, little missy; that does it for to-day. Let's get you back to class."

fter Orienteering Club, me and the other kids walked to the parking lot to catch our rides home. Mr. Chris walked out, too, heading towards his car. He paused for a minute, watching kids leave, making sure everyone got out all right, not wanting to see anyone left behind. One by one, the other kids left. I didn't see Mom or her car anywhere.

Mr. Chris came over to me, looking concerned that I was the only one left.

I was starting to get upset. Mr. Chris asked, "Why don't we call? Maybe she's just running a bit behind." He took out his phone and punched a few numbers, waited. No answer. Only to voice mail. "Good afternoon, Stacy. It's Mr. Long, Abbie's coach and counselor. We're here in the school parking lot and wondering if you're running late. If you could give me a call back once you get this message, I'd appreciate it." He hung up.

I was so embarrassed I wanted to crawl under a rock. Why did he have to make an issue out of it? "Don't worry, Mr. Chris. I'll just walk home. I like walking sometimes."

He didn't look convinced. "Tell you what," he said. "You have an emergency contact, right?" I nodded. "Should I go in and look it up in your file?"

"It's my friend Megan's mom. Her name is Rachel Rodriguez. I've got her number here in my phone. It's even labeled ICE."

"In case of emergency. Good. I wish all my students would do that so we'd know who to call if they couldn't talk. Give me your phone and I'll give her a call."

"I can call her," I said, wishing Mr. Chris would just go away and let me deal with the situation myself.

"I'd like to speak to her and make sure she can come and get you." I handed over my phone.

He pushed the icon to call her. After a few moments, Rachel answered. "Hello? Mrs. Rodriguez?"

Pause. He explained the situation to her, they said goodbye, hung up. "Abby, Mrs. Rodriguez is on her way over to pick you up. It'll just take a minute; I'll just hang out with you for a bit and make sure you get the ride you need."

"I'll be OK, Mr. Chris. You don't need to wait." I sincerely hoped no one would see him standing with me, like I was a lost little kid or something. He wasn't budging.

"I know you don't need me to wait, but it's happening anyway, so relax. You'll be home soon. Let's talk about maps."

Sheesh. We didn't seem to have trouble talking in his office or at the club meetings. Now, it was more personal—and embarrassing. Maps it was.

～⁓⁓〇

After Mrs. Rodriguez arrived, I waved at Mr. Chris and got into her Buick LeSabre, a sort of maroonish geeky car with the big Buick grill in front. The inside was quiet once the doors were closed. She played some soft classical elevator music, and I sunk deeper into the seats. We exchanged pleasantries, but neither of us really knew what to say.

We pulled up to the curb in front of our house. There it was—Mom's car, just sitting in the driveway. Guess she forgot. Again.

"Do you want to me walk you in?" she asked.

Oh, man. Could this be more humiliating? What am I, like six? "I'll be fine. Thank you for driving me home."

"It's fine. Anytime you need me, Abby, just call. See you soon." I nodded and got out, shutting the car door. She stayed parked as I walked up the sidewalk to the front door. I unlocked it, opened the door, then looked back at Megan's Mom. Go away now.

I walked inside and shut the door, dropping my back in the foyer. I looked into the living room and saw exactly what I expected to see: Mom was passed out on the couch, the usual glass bottles and tissues on the coffee table.

Enough. I walked over to the couch, leaned over so that my mouth was right by her ear, and shouted, "Mom!"

Mom jumped about nine feet. Then she slowly turned to look at me. Wow—she looked like shit. She looked like the walking dead, or maybe the barely shuffling dead. "Abbie! What the hell?" She looked up at the clock and saw the time. Realization dawned over her face. "Baby, I am so sorry. Come here." She reached out to me. Looking for brains to eat, no doubt. I stared at her for a minute, then turned and stomped upstairs.

"Sweetheart, wait!" Mom cried. She tried to stand up and stumbled, almost falling over. I could hear her starting to sob, talking to herself. "I'm so sorry. I'm so sorry."

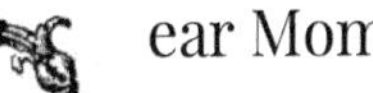

ear Mom:

So I got this assignment, to write this letter. I thought about it a lot before starting, and I'm not sure where it's going to end. Since no one will probably ever read it, I guess I'm just going to write out some of what I've been thinking and feeling.

I'm kind of resentful that I have to do this at all. More homework is going to help? More spending time alone without you or Dad or anyone else? Sounds sucky to me. But I do as I'm told. Sometimes I wish I were a bad girl that just disobeyed and did whatever I felt like. That's not really in me.

So here I am, writing this letter to the person who has let me down over and over.

I'm just sorry that it ended up being you.

You've always been something that I've strived to be. Beautiful, and smart, kind and ambitious. I was kind of jealous about how Dad felt about you, and delighted watching you with your own dad, my Grandpa whom I love to pieces. I wanted to be you when I grew up. That's a lot of pressure to put on a girl. Sometimes I wanted you to be less than perfect, so that there wouldn't be so much to live up to. I'm sorry I got what I wanted.

I also wanted to be perfect because you're a terror when you're mad. I never want you to be angry with me. You're scary, you know?

The problem with that is that trying to make you not angry has made me angry. Like all the time. I'm so angry my thoughts are like a pile of worms. I'm not doing well in school, and I can't have fun with my friends like I used to.

I know it wasn't always perfect between you and Grandpa. I know it was hard living with a vet who fought in Vietnam. But you figured that out. Why can't you figure out how to live with Dad fighting, too? If you didn't want him to go away, why did you marry a soldier in the first place?

I know that it's hard for you. You have had to make a lot of sacrifices for our family, and I admire you for that. It's another reason that I wanted to be just like you.

I guess that's why it hurts now, when you let me down, again and again.

But you know what? I've learned something all by myself. This is something you didn't teach me. I taught me this. Being angry is getting me nowhere. Fast. And I'm tired of it.

I can't think of any way to get beyond angry, except for one thing. I have to forgive you. Not for your sake, but for mine. I have more to offer this world than my anger.

I forgive you.

Abbie

16

e didn't talk the rest of the night. When I was getting ready for bed, there was a knock at my door.

"Abbie? Can I come in?" asked Mom. She cracked open the door and peaked in. "Abbie? Sweetie." She came in and sat down next to me. "I feel absolutely horrible. I can't say that I'm sorry enough."

I didn't know if I could talk any more. There was so much to say, and it seemed none of it would do any good. "You're not the only one who feels bad that Dad isn't here. I think about it every day. I almost cry every day I think about him."

"I know, baby girl. I just…"

"I'm not dumb, you know. I know that you and Grandpa had problems a long time ago, but now it seems fine. Why can't we be fine?"

"It's not like that, sweetie."

"Then tell me. What's it like?"

She didn't really answer. "It's just really hard. We're both scared."

"But you forgot me. You've been forgetting about me. It's like I'm not even here." I was not going to let her off the hook. Not get away with telling me not to worry.

"I know. I'm so sorry. I will make it up to you. I will make it right."

"What does that even mean?"

Mom got up to leave. I guess she didn't have an answer. I was ready to let her go, and then remembered what Mr. Chris and I had discussed. I guess I had to go through with it.

Why not? I really didn't have anything left to lose. "Mom?"

"Yes?"

"I love you."

Mom stopped in the doorway. She didn't turn back to me, but as she walked away, I heard, "I love you, too."

Mom was in the kitchen, pacing as she talked on the phone. She was in the middle of a heated conversation. "I don't know how many times I have to tell you. My husband is deployed. I have given you the sponsor ID three times now." She paused. "We've been covered since he's been in. It makes no sense how we just fall off."

"He can't just..." Her frustration boiled over. "He's in Iraq! How the hell do you expect him to walk in and fix this? You still haven't told me..."

"No. Thanks for nothing." She slammed the phone onto the counter and let out a frustrated scream. The phone rang again. She stormed out. I didn't feel like answering it, either.

17

hen combat veterans come home, they tell stories. They tell those stories to each other, maybe not even realizing that children are listening. These stories don't sound real. They sound like a baseball highlight reel: Here are the amazing heroic catches; here's the home run I hit; here's the blooper you made. There's little or nothing of the time in between. Standing on deck, striking out, waiting on base for someone else's at bat. Or even waiting around for the other team to show up. Remember, you can't have a war if the other team doesn't fight back.

The player and the soldier, though, they both have the same goal. Safe at home.

We all tell stories, I guess, especially when we're trying to make sense of things that are senseless. Having a beginning, middle, and happily-ever-after gives meaning to the meaningless. It's almost impossible to go through something traumatic and come out the other side with a working brain unless there's some sort of meaning to it all. So they tell stories, and don't always think about who might be listening.

My dad told stories about his time at war. Not many to me. Some to my grandpa, since he had been a soldier in his turn. Some more to the guys he knew who had been there. I listened. And I put together a tale—an attempt to find meaning.

This part of the story starts with a bang. A loud one. A rocket-propelled grenade had exploded, knocking my dad flat on his back. When he reached down to his leg, his hand came back bloody. My father, the paladin with the lion heart, pulled himself up, got behind a vehicle for cover, and then began returning fire.

He wasn't concerned about this little bit of blood. He had a magic talisman, the enchanted bracelet that he believed would keep him bulletproof. And he had his band of men, the ones who had his back—the ones who would never let him down.

He looked around, but he couldn't see any of his men where he needed them to be, providing covering fire so he could move out of the open with only this one vehicle between him and certain death. Where had they gone?

He saw his right-hand man, his shield, his best hope lying down in the street beyond the vehicle's protection. Another soldier tried to get him, to lift him up and carry him to safety, but he was hit and fell dead beside Rodriguez.

My knight-warrior-dad left his somewhat position and ran to the man he trusted most. He saw where a bullet had hit, tearing through his body armor. He dragged him back, limping, to the vehicle, where he pressed down on the hole, putting pressure to stop the bleeding. He saw his hands become covered with blood and dirt and other unmentionables as his hands sunk deeper into Megan's dad's body. Rodriguez had a bracelet, too. Had the magic gone?

The blood started to cover Dad's bracelet. Now it was all one color; the coded message erased.

18

lthough I didn't know the details of that story at the time, I knew the ultimate outcome. Because I was there when Megan got the news.

Megan and I were playing *Where in the World is Carmen Sandiego* upstairs in her room. To play, you had to answer trivia questions that allowed you to move around the world—on the game's board, naturally. Somehow, the Golden Gate Bridge had been stolen and we had to help. I answered my question and moved my V.I.L.E. Henchman five spaces. We heard a crash, something falling, and then a soft scream. We both jumped up and ran out of the room.

We scampered downstairs and saw the front door standing open. In front of it, Megan's mom stood, keeping herself upright by holding onto the table in the foyer. There was an Army officer standing there in a Class A uniform. Megan and I looked at each other, trying to decipher what his presence meant.

Rachel saw us and beckoned to Megan. "Come here, baby..."

Megan still looked confused as she slowly walked towards her mother, who pulled her in tight. I could see it in Megan's face—the exact second when her heart broke. There was such an intimate pain between Megan and her mom that I felt like I shouldn't be there at all. I looked away, noticing the broken vase that had fallen from the table supporting them.

I started to crumble a little bit, too. He must be a Casualty Notification Officer. My mind was all mixed up. I was crushed for Megan, sad because I liked her dad and he was my father's friend, worried in case another one of these ghouls was at my house at this very second, embarrassed if they showed up and all they found was my mom, drunk. Kind of happy that it wasn't my house, and maybe wouldn't be. Our dads served together, right? Did that make it more likely or less likely that Dad was hit, too?

Another man stepped forward. Must be the chaplain. He put his hand on Rachel's shoulder, but she shook it off. He tried again, and this time it stuck.

All I could hear was the phrase echoing through my head, "The Secretary of the Army has asked me to share with you his deepest regrets…"

I softly said, "I'm so sorry," as I passed by then ran home at full speed.

❧

The day of the funeral was sunny and beautiful, with a whisper of wind and a clear sky. The air was suffocating.

Flags surrounded St. Albert the Great Catholic Church on Bittern Hollow as hundreds of people—including many students—attended the service for Corporal Rodriguez. The Pflugerville school district had let out classes for the day so everybody could pay their respects. The church was nice. They did some services in Spanish, which I know the Rodriguez family liked, and Megan was hoping to have her quinceañera there. Now she didn't even know if they were going to stay in Austin. She and her mom might have to move to be closer to other family. I wanted her to stay right here. Somehow, the media had been kept out of the church service and grounds, so it wasn't the zoo it could have been. The priest told a few stories and talked about the decorated soldier's faith that supposedly kept him going while he was fighting overseas.

It all seemed rather cold to me. It would have been better if one of his friends could have talked, but I guess they were all still overseas keeping-going-through-their-faith.

Along with the Travis County Sheriff's Department, Patriot Guard riders led the processional to Our Lady of the Rosary Cemetery in Georgetown. Once we got there, we saw a funeral detail in dress uniform pulling the flag-draped coffin out of the hearse and then walking in step to the grave site.

We made our way over there, too, with all the other people. Next to the site itself, someone had put up an easel and on it was a big blown-up picture of Damion.

The honor guard rifle team presented their 21-gun salute, firing three shots in unison, and then there was a recording of *Taps.* The flag got folded up, the men very precise in their movements. Once it was in a tight triangle, one soldier knelt in front of Rachel. She was sitting very close to Megan, the two practically leaning on each other. Mom grabbed my hand and we both squeezed tight.

He presented the folded flag with the long straight edge facing Rachel. He said, "On behalf of the President of the United States, the United States Army, and a grateful nation, please accept this flag as a symbol of our appreciation for your loved one's honorable and faithful service." Megan's mom sat there, stunned. I think she was cried out.

I think Mom was thinking that she could have been the one sitting there. I found the whole even morbid— and terrifying.

19

hen Mom and I got home from the funeral, I saw our boxes of Christmas decorations sitting stacked, ready to be opened and put on display. They looked unspeakably sad. I couldn't bear any more; I ran upstairs to my room, leaving Mom alone downstairs.

The phone rang. Mom answered it, and after a fake-chipper "Hello?" she came completely unglued. I crept downstairs to try and overhear what was happening. I peeked around the corner into the kitchen, where Mom was on the phone, struggling to talk, sobbing.

"It's Daddy," she mouthed to me. She put the phone on speaker.

"Hey, Dad."

"Hey, princess. How are you?"

"I'm OK. How are you?"

"I'm good, baby," he answered. "You guys put up the Christmas tree yet?"

"No, not yet." Why were we talking about Christmas? Doesn't he know where we just were? He must. He must know why Mom is crying, why my answers are so short.

"How's school going?"

"It's OK." Like I gave two craps about school right now.

"That's it? Just OK? There has to be something good going on..."

"We're getting ready for a Christmas play. We're doing a Charlie Brown Christmas. I'm playing Lucy." The psychiatrist is in. You owe me five cents.

"That's awesome. I wish I could be there to see it."

"It's OK."

"Well, listen. I need to talk to your mom about a few things. You keep being you and kick butt being Lucy. I love you so much."

"I love you too, Dad. I miss you."

"I miss you, baby girl."

Mom took the phone off the speaker setting and pressed it to her face. I started to leave the kitchen, but I didn't get far. I was definitely going to eavesdrop on this one.

"Oh, my god! How bad?

"And they're not going to send you back home?

"I don't care. Any wound should be enough to send you home.

"You better not have made the choice to stay on your own." Oh, yeah, I'm sure he can't wait to get back here, to the crazy house.

"I'm sorry, it just scares the hell out of me to know that you're hurt and they're just going to send you back out there." He must have said something that sounded good to Mom. She was calming down, breathing easier.

"Please just be careful and come back, I don't think I could live through what I saw today." What about Megan and Megan's mom? You don't seem to think about maybe they could use help getting through this.

"I love you too. So much," she croaked out before hanging up. I leaned against the wall, knowing what had happened. Nothing for me to do here even if I could think of anything to do. I went back upstairs. The usual. Me upstairs, her downstairs with a bottle.

The next morning, I left my bedroom, ready for school. My parent's bedroom door is open and the bed is still made. I went downstairs towards the kitchen.

Mom was passed out on the couch. The coffee table is filthy. I don't even care anymore. I don't want her driving me anywhere. It was cold, so I grabbed my warm coat, gloves, and knit hat and out I went. Thank goodness she was gone when I came home. Maybe I'd have time to put up some Christmas stuff. I was guessing she wouldn't have time in her busy schedule.

I managed to put up the wreath and the holder for Christmas cards, if anyone sent them this year. I kind of lost heart for the endeavor and started on my homework. About a half an hour later, the phone rang.

"Hello?"

"Hey." It was Megan.

"What's up?"

"Um, well, your mom was here for a visit. I guess she wanted to cheer up my mom or something."

"That's nice, I guess."

"Yeah, nice." Megan hesitated. "It's just that she kind of had a few while she was here."

Ah.

"Did your mom say anything?"

"Well, she asked your mom if she was OK to drive. Your mom said she was."

"Was she?"

"I'm not sure. I just thought I should let you know, in case she's late or something, you could maybe call someone? I didn't know what to do."

Like I know what to do. "Yeah, thanks. I'm sorry."

"You don't have to be sorry, Abbie. See you tomorrow?"

"Yeah, OK. Thanks for calling." I hung up, having no idea what I was supposed to do. I paced and thought. Who could I call?

After an eternity, I picked up the phone.

"Hello?"

"Grandpa?"

"Abbie? It's late. Is everything all right?"

"No. Mom's supposed to be home. She left my friend's house over an hour ago. It's ten minutes away, max. I don't know what to do."

"Sweetheart, stay where you are and I'll be right over."

Grandpa pulled into the empty driveway, got out, and headed to the door. I came out and met him. "I want to stay with you tonight," I said.

"Of course. Let's pack you a bag." I grabbed some random stuff while he got on the phone, trying to find my Mom I suppose. I didn't even want to know. I just wanted out of there. We left, locking the door behind us. After we got to his house, Grandpa said, "Can I get you something to drink? Afraid I only have water and orange juice."

"Water, please."

"Grab a seat on the couch," he said. "I'll be right in."

I dropped my bag on the couch, but I couldn't sit still. I paced some more, just like I was doing at home.

Different things to see here, though. Old family pictures on the walls. A shadow box of military ribbons and ranks and stuff. I stopped, looking them over.

Grandpa walked back in with a glass of water. He handed it to me. "You know, it wasn't much easier for your grandmother either. Of course, Vietnam was a very different time."

"How so?"

He pulled me over to the couch with him. Maybe I could sit for a while. "Well, many of us were forced to go. We didn't know how long we'd be there and when we came home, many people hated us."

"Why?"

"They didn't understand. So many things were changing in the sixties. People were angry at the government, at authority, at the world, really. They wanted someone to be angry at and we were just an easy target."

"What happened between you and Mom?" I asked. "She never talks about it."

"Remember that last bit about coming home? It was really hard on me. I couldn't handle it. I couldn't understand why I was hated. I lost friends over there, too. Wasn't easy. I began drinking…"

"…like Mom."

"Yes, but I was much worse. It took me a long time to realize what I was doing. If it wasn't for your grand-mother, I might not have ever gotten better."

"Grandma helped?"

"She saved my life, sweetheart," he said. "And from the moment I understood what I was doing, I knew that I needed to change—and did."

"I don't understand. Why didn't mom see that? If she saw you change, why doesn't she?"

He sighed. "To be honest, she learned the bad part from me. I guess she didn't understand the better part, even though she's a big reason why I changed. But I promise you, I will do everything I can to help, and we'll get your mom back. She loves you deeply, she just really needs our help right now."

"How can I help? Nothing I do seems to make much difference."

"I don't know right now, Abbie. I have to figure out how she got to where she is and then figure out how we move forward."

"Where is she?"

"Abbie, she's in jail."

20

ad couldn't just come home. First, we had to go back to the base auditorium for more speeches and Texas glad-handing.

"Good afternoon! This is the meeting we've all been waiting for. It's been a long fourteen months with a roller coaster of emotions, but the time has finally come for us to welcome our soldiers home!" said Lauren, the up-with-deployment cheerleader.

She paused for some applause from the spring-butts in the audience. They were the excited families; some, like Mom and me, were more subdued. Then Lauren beamed and continued, "We have all had to change our lives and make adjustments to our daily routines to keep our families going during this time. It's been difficult for all of us, but because of this, we will now have to go through another phase of adjustment. Our soldiers have had to change their lives also, and getting them integrated into our new and different routines will be challenging. We want to help you all through this challenge."

One the pep-talked had droned out, Grandpa headed to the bleachers to save us some seats and get away from the milling bodies. Mom and I walked over to the tables that looked like they'd been in place since the Pleistocene. Homecoming adjustment fliers adorned the tabletops. Nothing new, really. As we turned away, Lauren was right behind us like a sprightly shadow.

"Stacy Matthews, right?" asked Lauren. "And you must be Abbie." Yes, I must.

"Yes," Mom acknowledged.

"I know that you and Rachel are good friends, and I just wanted to ask how she was doing." Oh, Lauren, right. You know all about this coming-home drill, but maybe not so much about the not-coming-home part.

"I haven't really talked to her much since the funeral," admitted mom. "Wanted to give her some space. Especially now." *No, you didn't, liar. You didn't want to think about anyone but yourself.*

"Yeah, I can't imagine it being easy for them hearing about the rest of the battalion coming home," said Lauren. "How is your family holding up?" *She magnanimously included me. No one asked about Megan.*

"We're good. Just trying to make it until Aaron returns."

"You know, it's going to take a few months for things to really settle. I heard that he and Damion were close. He's probably going to blame himself, so that's something you should be ready for."

"Thank you, I'll keep that in mind."

Lauren moved closer to my mother, as if some big secret was about to be revealed. I made sure that I remained within earshot, but not making eye contact. Like being around a skittish horse you don't want to bolt. "One more thing. I know what you're going through, and I know someone who can help. They are very discreet and he runs the meetings out of his home."

Mom acted all surprised, like she didn't know what Lauren was talking about. "I'm sorry?"

"The bags under the eyes, slightly glossed over, red cheeks. I've been there myself. I know the signs. I just want to help before Aaron gets home. Trust me—ignoring it will only make the transition harder."

And trust me, little-miss-chicken, you just didn't do anything to help. And I have to go home with her, not you. Thanks a million.

Mom had had enough. "Look, your husband might be my husband's commander, but that doesn't make you my boss. Why don't you worry about your family and I'll worry about mine. Thanks for your concern, but with all due respect, mind your own business."

Mom turned and stormed away. Lauren looked down at me as if I'd have some answers. I glared at her, then turned and followed Mom.

Sorry, Lauren. I'm the family secret keeper until Dad comes home.

"So that's exciting!" said Mr. Chris.

"I'm actually nervous about it." My dad was coming home!

"Well, it's been a really long time. It's perfectly normal to feel nervous."

"I've almost forgotten what he looks like. I mean, I have pictures, and I see them every day, but it's different when he's actually there. Hearing him talk and laugh, seeing his smile."

"It seems as if you are going to meet him all over again. Just think about it like that. You've grown up a lot since he's been gone, so both of you might have changed a bit. Be ready to learn some new things about each other, and if it helps, write about them. And don't be afraid to communicate your feelings to him."

21

We headed on up to the bleachers, which were filled with families and welcome-home signs. We took seats where Grandpa had secured some prime real estate. Lots of mumbly conversations in the crowd. I felt like shouting nonsense again. I heard a snippet of a political conversation about gun control. Here of all places: A welcome home event in Texas. I heard that old chestnut, "Guns don't kill people, people kill people."

In my mind, I yelled out, "And toasters don't toast...the toasted toast toast!"

I think I have forgotten how to breathe.

Then, silence, and from the corner of the bleachers, the lead company marched the battalion onto the field, NCOs calling the instep cadence. The crowd erupted and everyone jumped to their feet.

Once the battalion had reached its position, the Standing O started to dissipate. LTC Reading—a.k.a. Lauren's husband—approached the podium.

Colonel Reading began, "It gives me great pleasure to be standing in front of you today welcoming home your soldiers. I can tell you that there isn't a prouder moment for a company commander." He paused. "I would, however, like to take a moment of silence to reflect and remember those that paid the ultimate sacrifice to their country and the cause of freedom."

The crowed hushed into silence.

"Thank you. Once your soldiers have been released from formation, you will all have twenty minutes together, then we must take them back for just a little bit to do leave paperwork, and then they are all yours! Command Sergeant Major, the battalion is yours."

"Battalion! Company!"

The NCOs echoed him to their smaller units, and the mass formation broke apart. The families poured out of the bleachers. In the collision of happiness, it looked like it would take 20 minutes just to find Dad.

Happy hugs, children screaming, crying. I took off towards Dad's part of the dissolving formation.

I collided with him in a running jump into his arms, knocking off his booney. Mom paraded up to us, and Dad turned to her. They wasted no time locking lips. Grandpa eased over, and looked at me after seeing their deep kissing.

I looked up at him. "Yuck."

They stopped. Dad looked at us with a big, goofy grin. He laughed and said, "Sorry."

"It's OK." I grabbed his neck in a big hug. "But only this once."

Grandpa moved in to hug Dad. As they separated and looked each other in the eye, Gramps seemed to see something wasn't quite right. Dad broke eye contact first, and laughed again, a little more nervous this time. He kissed me on the forehead and we all hugged as a family.

It would all be all right now. Dad was home.

In the car, we were all together again. There was no conversation. It was like no one knew how to start talking. Mom and Dad gave each other little smiles, but it didn't look natural. He looked back at me but I was making sure to studiously examine the fascinating countryside.

When he was looking back at the road, I snuck a peek at him. His face was so focused. His grip on the steering wheel tightened, in response to something I couldn't see. Mom took a turn gazing out the window, her fingers drumming out a complex pattern against her leg. Her nerves were shot.

So were mine.

⌘

Once Dad pulled into the driveway, we got out and slammed the car doors and walked inside. Mom and I did our usual enter-and-split, me upstairs, Mom to the kitchen. Neither of us considered doing something other than what we did every other day.

Dad had stopped right inside the door, watching us walk away. He dropped his duffle bag and breathed deeply. He looked around, and noticed he was standing alone.

"Hey! Where is everyone going?" I froze halfway up the stairs. Mom turned and peered out from the kitchen. Dad continued, "I think a celebration is in order! What do you say we go out?"

Mom and I both turned back and walked like zombies back to the foyer. I don't think that's what Dad was expecting. He had no idea how exhausted we were, how drained from emotion and secrets and distrust.

"Well, let's not everyone jump at once!" Mom and I just looked at him. "Ok, well, I'm going to go change real quick since this is all I've worn over the past fifteen months." He gives them both a confused look and goes to change.

Mom just picked up her purse and stood there, transfixed.

22

e went back to The Roaring Fork. We'd had lots of fun family meals here, but this was not one of them.

Each time I looked up from my food, it was at the exact second that my parents decided to look down at their food. If Mom looked towards Dad, he looked towards me, and I looked back at my food. I looked at Mom, she took a sip of wine. Dad looked like a prisoner eating. He didn't once let his hand off of his water glass. Like someone would take it right out from under his nose.

I think I brushed my hair back with my hand a hundred times. If I ate my napkin, no one would have said boo—assuming they even noticed.

Somehow, we made it through, and the check was paid. We got back into the car for the ride home. Still no one was talking. I felt hyperaware, like I'd notice if someone's breathing changed or a bug hit the windshield. Dad was getting more and more tense, squeezing harder on the steering wheel. His gaze intensified until he zoned onto a pair of lights from an oncoming car. He cocked his head like he heard something in the silence. Mom turned away from the passenger window and grabbed the steering wheel. "Aaron!" she screamed. "Oh, my god!" She jerked the wheel away from Dad's death grip.

The car screeched and flew side to side. I was holding on for dear life and my eyes were locked shut. My stomach was flopping around like a fish on dry land. Then still. Somehow, we had gotten to the side of the road, full-stop.

We were all looking at each other, terrified. Our eyes flitted back and forth, at each other, at the road, at the car, at the floor. None of us knew what to do.

Then Mom made a decision. "I'm driving the rest of the way home," she said.

Mom and dad quietly exited their respective doors and switched sides. Their quiet calm scared me more than if they were screaming at each other. Is this the next thing we're going to pretend is normal?

I sat in shock the rest of the way home.

I finally managed to fall asleep. In the middle of the night, I woke, not sure what had jostled me out of slumberland. I lay there in the darkness, listening hard for some kind of noise—something that had meaning. Then I heard a sound I wish never had existed in this world.

Dad. Screaming. Terrible, haunting, haunted. I could hear him spring out of bed, but no conversation. I couldn't hear Mom at all.

I heard Dad stumble to the bathroom.

Once upon a time they were going to grow old together. It sounded like now they had decided to fall apart together.

23

I went with Dad to the Austin VA, which smells like pee. That's where he has to go, even though it's really obnoxious there. You have to wait forever for anything and they always lose stuff and make you feel really small. Like it's there because of veterans, not there for veterans, if you follow that.

The place is supposed to open at 7:30 in the morning, but that's just when people start arriving. While you sit there, they stumble in, turn on their computers, wait for them to boot up. Maybe get a cup of coffee. Ignore the room full of soldiers looking for some kind of help.

The system is so stupid. My dad called to make an appointment, and they told him he couldn't make an appointment until he was assigned to a doctor. But in order to be assigned to a doctor, he had to come in. Without an appointment. Just sit there until someone gets around to you. With all the other soldiers doing the same thing.

My Dad was wearing his uniform and filling out paperwork on a clipboard like you do at every doctor's office everywhere.

Finally, after close to two hours, a nurse announces, "Staff Sergeant Matthews, Aaron?"

He looked up uneasily and stood to follow the nurse. He came back out. All done. He was with the doctor for four minutes. He looked so sad as we left to drive home.

⁓‿‿⌁

A few days later, Dad and Grandpa took me to the shooting range. I love it there. And no, it's not odd for someone my age to go. In Texas, it's pretty common for kids to have learned at least the basics of firearms usage. The idea is that just telling a kid, "This is a gun—never touch it" will pretty much guarantee that they will touch it at some point. And kids are used to video games where what they shoot gets right back up again. Instead, starting children early on firearm safety and when they're ready, what it's really like to shoot, teaches them safety protocols and respect for the weapon.

Besides, it's completely fun.

I like to go because, like I said, it's fun, but also because they're hyper about hearing protection. That's great for obvious reasons, but the sneaky reason is that adults talk there and figure no one can hear what they say, even though they're practically shouting since they can't hear themselves very well. I wait for the Cease Fire call and then listen in. You learn all sorts of stuff that the adults weren't intending.

Dad and Grandpa decided that they were going to fire handguns, and stood side-by-side facing the targets down range. After one iteration, they returned to the loading table for more ammo.

"This is the best kind of therapy," Dad declared.

"You're not wrong," Grandpa replied, not noticing me behind them. He looked at Dad and continued, "So, how are you holding up?"

"Hm? Oh, I'm good."

"That's not very convincing."

"What, are you going to interrogate me at the range?" asked Dad.

"It's not an interrogation, Aaron. It's a question. One you should answer honestly."

My dad stopped loading the magazine, giving in to the question. "Ok. Well, I can't shake Damien's dead body out of my head, and no matter how many times I wash my hands, I still see his blood on them. I wake up in the middle of the night screaming, scaring the whole house, and to top it all off, I've got a drug store on my kitchen counter with a bunch of crap that only makes me zone out."

"Are you talking to anybody?"

"What? You mean at the VA? Ha! They gave me their default PTSD cocktail. They checked that box."

"Can't argue with you there," said Grandpa. "But listen. You're not just a son-in-law to me. You're a brother. I've been in your situation, and in Stacy's, too. You have to trust me in that the deeper you two dig that hole, the harder it is to climb out. Don't be ashamed to lean on me when you need to, Aaron. We're all we got."

Dad listened. Then he got it—and so did I. Where Mom had been. Maybe finally Mom would have to listen, too.

24

 sat on the couch in Dr. Chris' office. "He's just different. I dunno. He doesn't talk much, him and mom fight a lot. He had nightmares, too. I hear him scream sometimes."

"What about you?" he asked. "Are you still having nightmares?"

"No. They stopped when he came back."

"Well, that's a good thing. Have you and your dad spent any time together since he's been back?"

"Not really. We go out to eat sometimes, but that's not fun anymore."

"In what way is it not fun?"

"Everyone just sits there. No one talks." I looked down at my bracelet.

After we got back home, I went upstairs to take a shower and wash off the heat and dust of the range. When I came out, Mom and Dad were at it. It's always so embarrassing to listen to other people fight. It's worse than watching two people make out, you know?

I could hear them down in the kitchen, they were yelling so loud. "How long?" screamed my dad.

"Does it matter? What do you care?" Dad must have found Mom's pill stash, or maybe some hidden bottles. Didn't really matter.

"Christ, Stacy. You would think that after growing up with your father, you would have learned. Had it been this bad the whole time? You went to jail? How could you put our daughter in a position like that? Yeah, Mom. How?

"How dare you question me like a child."

"That's what you're missing, Stacy!" he yelled. "A child! You are forgetting that you have one!"

"And you aren't? You think your little outbursts are helping at all?" Dad made a sound like he'd been punched in the gut. "You zone out and aren't even there. You're like a zombie, and it's as if you never came back. What the hell else am I supposed to do?"

Dad's voice is calm now. It's actually creepier than when he was yelling. "Do you have any clue what it's like? No. You don't. I feel like a crazy person constantly doped up on all of this crap." He reaches down picking up one of the pill bottles and slams it back down. "If you knew..."

She cut him off. "...If I knew? What do you know? Having to do everything, having to deal with your daughter slowly losing her mind while you're gone, not knowing if you'll ever come back, watching Rachel bury her husband. Then watching you lose your mind?"

"Don't put that on me! I spent fifteen months living everyday not knowing if it's going to be my last, getting blown up, and then watching my best friend die!" I heard a crash. A bottle had smashed against the wall. "Drink yourself stupid for all I care." At that he stormed out of the house. I don't know where he went. And I don't know what Mom did. I just lay on my bed, wishing myself to turn to stone. My whole body jumped when Dad slammed the front door.

I didn't think I'd get any sleep after that, but I must have dozed off because I jolted awake when my alarm went off. Joy—another day at school. I cleaned up and dress, grabbed my bag, and as I left my room I looked over at my parent's bedroom. The door was closed. I walked past it and headed downstairs.

In the living room, my mom was passed out on the couch. Tissues littered the coffee table. Fine—things were back to normal. Figuring I would walk to school again, I went into the kitchen for a Pop-Tart and my backpack. I heard someone walking downstairs behind me. Must be Dad. School could wait. I wanted to hear what happened next.

Dad must have sat near her, as he kept his voice low. "I'm sorry about last night."

"I want a divorce." Straight to the point. That's Mom.

"Wha...What? Why?"

"Why do you think? I can't do this anymore. I spent the past year and three months stressed to no end, worried about you. You know how many times Abbie had walked to school because I'm passed out on the couch?" Could she even hear herself? She was so worried. She had no choice but to get drunk and pass out so I had to walk to school and its Dad's fault. And of course no mention of what I was feeling. I was just a bit of inconvenience.

Mom kept talking. "We've already lost each other, and we're losing our daughter. It has to end before we all go more crazy than we already are." She waited for a response. "For Christ sake, say something."

"I d...I don't know what you want me to say. I don't know what to say." Dad stood up, pacing. "I know things haven't been great, but it's all changed. I've already lost my best friend and part of my sanity, and now my family? I just can't..." he trailed off.

"How can you not see that we are too far gone? I can't handle any more."

I have no idea what Mom expected him to do. She had given him no options. She couldn't handle any more, but she could handle losing him? Losing me? I guess I was just another problem she couldn't handle.

Not wanting any part of this world they were destroying, I snuck out, trying to get out of there and get to school. I heard a crash coming from the garage. I ran in, worried about what was happening now, and there was Dad, an empty table in front of him, and tools and hardware strewn everywhere. He must have dumped it all. I was terrified.

He grabbed a hammer from the wall and turned and threw it without even looking. It crashed inches from my head, hitting a shelf that held our fishing equipment. The gear came tumbling down, some of it tumbling down on me.

He crumbled. He sat on the garage floor, his head in his hands.

I went to school.

After sitting through hours of numbness, I rifled through my backpack, looking for my math homework. Inside, I found one of the endless pamphlets they were always giving out at those military base functions. The title read, "Returning from the War

Zone: A Guide for Family of Military Members." I looked at it for a minute, then grabbed my bag and headed for the bathroom.

After reading it through, then reading it through again, I knew it was time. I ran to the guidance counselor's office and burst in, where she was sitting, talking on the phone to someone. She saw my face. "I have to go," she told the phone, and hung up. I don't know who she was talking to, and at that moment, I didn't care.

"We have to talk."

~⚬~

When I got home, I searched around for Dad. The only light I saw was in his study, which was a place I wasn't supposed to go unless absolutely necessary. Right now qualified.

I cracked open the door and snuck a look. He was sitting at his desk. The desk lamp was the only light in the room. His head was in his hands, again, and I could see a prescription bottle among the paperwork strewn over the desktop. He looked down and to his right, and his hand crept toward the top right drawer.

He slid it open and removed a manila folder, placing it on the desk. His hand went back to whatever had been under the folder. He slowly reached for it. Enough.

I shouldered the door open hard and moved toward him. "Daddy," I said with force.

His hand froze above the drawer. I looked into it and saw the handgun there. He slammed the drawer closed, and then turned to face me. Then he lost it.

It's not normal to see your Dad cry, I mean really sob, not those little tears when he's proud of you or whatever. I stood there, not knowing what to do. He collapsed to his knees and grabbed my legs, hugging them with force. I was a tree; I was stone. I couldn't hug back. The moment wasn't tender, and I was furious with him. And scared.

I would be strong. He didn't need another sobbing mess. I would be his strength, his armor.

"I'm sorry," he sobbed. I was silent.

"I love you so much."

"I know," I said. I was stone; I was his altar. I would not be weak. "I want you back."

He hitched a breath, and then calmed a bit.

I still didn't hug back. I'm not sure why. I didn't want to comfort him, to reward him for his atrocious behavior. I couldn't tell him his pain would stop, or the things that frighten him would go away. I didn't understand any of those things, so I couldn't promise him anything.

But no hugs from me. You will not move me by killing yourself. You will only move me by being strong. If you are not strong, take strength from me. I am a tree.

When his breathing was back to normal, he looked up at me. His eyes were calm.

"I want to go to the lake," I stated.

He smiled. "Yeah. Yeah. That would be great."

It was good. I hadn't saved his life. But I had given him the strength to save himself.

25

e pulled up to the parking area, just off of Pier 4. We sat in silence, looking out at the lake. Dad still had the steering wheel in a death-grip.

He was off on his own planet again. Time to bring him back to here and now, with me. "Dad?"

He snapped out of it. "Yeah." He opened his door, and so did I, climbing out of the truck and around back to help him offload the gear. While we were digging out the stuff, a familiar voice called out.

"Mind if I join you?"

Dad looked over his shoulder to see Grandpa walking up. He looked at me, confused. Then he turned back. "Tom. To what do I owe the surprise?"

The two big guys grasped hands. I ran to him and tackled him in a big hug. "Grandpa! You came!"

"Yeah, you two. Plotting something devious. What's going on?"

"I called him," I said.

Dad was trying hard not to look annoyed. "Not prepared for a third, but, sure. What brings you here?"

I handed Dad the last of the gear, and we started walking down the pier as Dad waited for Grandpa's explanation.

"Well, like Abbie said—she called me."

"About what?"

"Don't play dumb, Aaron. She's concerned."

I took the tackle box down the pier. I wanted them to have time to talk. I'd listen, naturally, but I knew they needed a little space to say what needed to be said.

Dad started, quietly. "Look. I don't know what this is, Tom, but..."

"Aaron, the last thing I want to do is intrude on your time with Abbie, but she reached out to me. You can't expect me to ignore that."

"Well, out with it."

"Aaron, I'm not the bad guy here. I'm also not a fool. You can try and wear that mask around everyone else, but I saw it in your eyes when you returned. And I saw it at the range. I'd hoped I had gotten through to you then." Dad just looked at him. "Abbie had matured beyond her years, and to be honest, it surprises me that someone her age handled what she's gone through as well as she had. It took an incredible amount of courage for her to call me last night."

"Last night?"

"Yes. Why?" Dad looked away, then toward me. I met his gaze straight on.

"Nothing."

"C'mon guys!" I cried. Men talk better when they're doing something—in this case, fishing. They started to walk down the pier. Their conversation was hushed, but still intense.

"Aaron. I know what you've been through and I see the wall that you've already built."

Dad said back, "I can't even begin to comprehend what it was like for you, but it doesn't change what happened." They stop.

"Don't you think I know that?"

"I meant no disrespect..."

"Frankly, I don't care," said Grandpa. "What I care about is you not taking the same road I did. You think you have it bad? When I came home, we were hated. We had rotten vegetables thrown at us. We were called the worst things imaginable. We'd survived only to come home to that.

"All I could think was *why didn't I die*? Why did they? What was it all for? I couldn't function any-more."

"Stacy's told me what happened."

"That's not the half of it. You know, even years later I tried to kill myself. I even failed at that. So I turned to the bottle and it destroyed me—my family. I lost my wife and almost lost my daughter. I fear that I still might."

Dad started to interrupt, but Grandpa held up a hand and shook his head. "It's what Stacy learned from me—try to numb the pain—drink it away."

They both looked towards me. Dad said, "I had my hand on the gun. I'd decided. What use was I if I was only driving them mad." He took a breath. "She saved my life, Tom. She may never know it, but it's what she did."

"Why do you think I sobered up? Why do you think we're having this conversation? Stacy saved mine."

The two of them had finished making their way to the end of the pier, sitting down next to me. I hadn't cast my line yet. I wasn't even sure that coming here was a good idea. I looked out over the water, hypnotized by the ripples and waves.

Dad tried to be light-hearted. "You gonna cast your line?"

"I know you and Mom are talking about getting divorced."

I could feel Dad's muscles contract, then release. He slouched down. "Sweetie, I'm not sure what you've heard, but..."

"What I hear is you two arguing all the time. You two never used to argue. Not like that."

Dad looked over at my grandpa who sat, listening. I continued, "I know that it was hard for you. I've read what I could find about what happened over there, and what it's like for some guys coming home, and I'm sorry that you had to go and see all of that. I know you changed, and that's OK. We all did."

I continued to look out at the lake as I talked. I paused, then turned to Dad. "I don't want you and mom to get divorced. Dad, she needs our help. You were supposed to be her knight-protector."

Dad didn't say anything. He looked over at Grandpa, who just sighed.

"What do we do?" Dad asked.

"She's right," said Grandpa. "But we have to be in this together. Accept that you need help. Be open to it. You are the same family—you just all have different perspectives now."

"I'm worried I'll only push her away further."

"No one said it would be easy. Believe me. If I could turn my hindsight now into foresight then, well—I can only imagine how different things would be." He looked at Dad, then down to me. "There've been enough casualties. This is something we can control."

Dad struggled to say what came next. "I couldn't save him. There was nothing I could do. I want to go back to that day so bad, I can't stop thinking about it. If I had done just one thing different, just one decision. A different route—maybe he'd still be alive."

I put my useless rod down and took his hand.

Grandpa said, "That can't be changed, and you know it. You can't predict every outcome. It's war. But you can't shoulder that burden alone, because then everyone else starts to bear that weight, not just you. You have to let go."

"I don't know how to do that."

My turn, I guess. I didn't know if anything I said would help. "I think it's forgiveness." They looked at me, surprised. "You have to forgive yourself, Dad. I forgive you and Mom."

Grandpa took up the theme. He sounded a little froggy. "She's right. It is the best way to start. Stacy needs her husband and this one needs her father." Dad and I looked each other in the eye. "And you need them both. The only way any of you can get through this is together."

Dad looked at me; gave me a little crooked grin. "I don't know, this one seems to be doing just fine." I smiled back, but with more uncertainty. I wasn't just fine at all. "This isn't going to be easy, Sweetheart. It's going to take a lot of work."

"I know. Do you think it's been easy up until now?" I shifted my weight. "You and Mom better figure this out before I get to High School, you know."

Dad smiled. "Oh yeah? Then I'd better get these in while I still can." He started kissing and tickling me. Seriously, I think I'm already too old for some of this. Or I will be tomorrow. Maybe I can be a silly girl for one more day.

"I love you, Dad. Mom does, too."

"I know she does, baby girl. I love the both of you more than you'll know."

~••~

The fish got a break that day, and none of them were coming home with us. After gathering up the gear, we plopped in into the truck bed. I gave Grandpa a hug and thanked him for coming out with us.

"I love you, Abbie," he said. I climbed into the passenger seat and shut the door. Grandpa walked over to my dad.

"Thanks again, Tom," he said. "It means a lot."

"Don't thank me. Look, I've been through it, and you can lean on me. I'm not just your father-in-law, I'm your brother, too." They clasped hands. "Abbie has one of the biggest hearts of anyone I've ever met. Just do her a favor and don't rely on her to be the glue. She is still just a little girl. She needs the two of you just as much as you need her. And don't give up on Stacy."

Dad nodded, and looked like he'd let go of a ten-ton weight. "I won't."

"Call me," said Grandpa. "We'll have dinner or go play bingo with all the other saps at the VFW."

"So I'm a sap now?"

"No, you're a combat veteran, like the rest of us. They could use some fresh young blood like you and the others. We have to be there for each other." He started to walk away, then turned to say one last thing through a half-smile. "Besides—combat bingo is surprisingly therapeutic."

Dad smiled back as Grandpa walked away, then turned and got into the truck. I smiled at him, tired and ready to call it a day. But then Dad said, "We have one stop to make before home." He put the truck in gear and off we went.

～⌣⌣〜

The stop ended up being the cemetery. Dad didn't know exactly where to go. There were a lot of stones there. But I had been there before, so I knew what he was looking for. I led him to the grave. Damion Rodriguez.

There was a wreath leaning against it, and sticking up from the ground is an American flag. Dad knelt down, staring at Damion's name.

"I didn't want to come here," Dad said. "I kept putting it off. I knew I should, I knew I had to, but I also knew once I was here I couldn't run any more. I couldn't keep pretending everything was fine, everything would have a storybook ending."

I understood. The stone was so concrete, so solid. Obvious. The person here is dead.

"I didn't want to accept that this man that I loved is gone."

"He's not feeling any pain, Dad." He looked up at me, with some shock in his eyes. "I know you're hurting, but he's not."

Dad nodded. He reached down to his wrist, where that bracelet I made him still sat. Cleaner, now, but still stained a bit red. He took it off. "Here, buddy. You need this more than I do."

Come home safe.

26

hat's what forgiveness is. Love. Love for yourself, for your family. Even when life is hard. You have to accept the past and forgive those that have hurt you, because otherwise you'll never have peace.

It's a lot easier to put a kid into a corner and punish them than it is to talk to them. But we understand way more than adults give us credit for. Sometimes you have to do what's right, even if it's hard. It's easier to give up and say that person is just bad. Forgiveness is not taking the easy way out.

When we lose the people we love, learning to move on is hard. But their memory can never die. Celebrate their lives and be happy that they were in yours to begin with.

It's easy to give up, and walk away when things get difficult, but it's harder to fight for what you love but worth it. Family is worth it. Fight for each other. Fight for love above all else.

People change all the time. It's how you let yourself change and what you do with that change that can make a difference in yourself and others.

Learn to forgive. Never forget to love.

Sometimes the hardest thing to do is to love each other. But it's the only thing that matters.

About the Author

Julia Dye tells stories because she loves to entertain and see a certain secret smile from her readers when she strikes a chord. She's spun stories of one kind or another since her childhood in Milwaukee, through college, and into a successful career in show business and publishing. Julia writes about everything that interests her, but she has an affinity for stories with a military flavor. Her Dad was a bomber pilot during World War II, and she married a Marine. She's won a Gold Medal from the Military Writers Society of America. Her tales ring true—which is a very cool thing for any author to claim.

She currently lives between Los Angeles, close to the entertainment business, and Lockhart, Texas, close to her heart.